Rain In O<

Published by Ink And Quill Press, 2024
Cover artwork by LeAnne Withrow

For more excellent works of fiction, visit
Inkandquillpress.com

Dedicated to my wife, Letisha, the enchanting, wonderful, beautiful woman who captured my heart all those years ago. Thanks for taking a chance on me. Here's to our happily ever after.

Chapter One

"Turn left, then turn left."

Helen didn't bother taking her eyes off the road to glance down at the dimly illuminated screen of her cellphone – her focus was solely on the torrential rain pounding against her windshield, obscuring her view of the highway ahead.

She squinted past her frantically waving wiper blades and tried desperately to distinguish the gray asphalt of Interstate 40 from the equally gray landscape of Oklahoma's waterlogged backcountry.

"Turn left, then turn left."

"Yes, thank you," she muttered to herself, glancing down to check her speed.

She was going ten under the limit, and hadn't seen more than a couple of cars in the last 50 miles and none in the past fifteen minutes. Not terribly unexpected. The middle of the afternoon on a Tuesday—not to mention in the middle of a massive storm cell—wasn't typically the busiest time to be out on the highway.

She'd timed this intentionally when she left Amarillo; she hated driving in congested traffic. She'd made sure she would be passing Oklahoma City after lunch but before evening rush hour. What she *hadn't* done was check the weather. She'd hit the rain just after the city, and conditions had steadily worsened over the past hour, leaving her here... wherever 'here' was.

Lightning flickered on a nearby hillside, briefly illuminating ugly, black-and-purple clouds and a landscape of wind-bent trees and rocky canyons.

Helen's knuckles turned white on the steering wheel as she realized that she was driving on a too-narrow road above a swollen, rushing creek.

This was most assuredly not I-40.

Risking a glance downward at the screen, she confirmed she was not on the interstate and had somehow managed to work her way onto a country road instead.

"Shit," she cursed herself and her lack of attention, a bead of sweat forming at the base of her neck.

She must've taken the wrong exit after Oklahoma City; no wonder no one else was on the road. She continued on a few more miles until she found a spot with at least some semblance of a shoulder to pull over onto, and then put her under-sized sedan in park. She turned the engine off as much out of habit as prudence - no point in wasting gas if she might be stretching it to get to the next open gas station.

Slender fingers with chewed, chipped fingernails pulled the smartphone from its place on the dash and brought it closer to her eyes, squinting behind thick, silver-rimmed glasses.

"Where the hell am I?"

She deftly navigated the device, expanding the map on its small screen and scrolling this way and that, comparing her former location to where she was and where she *should* be.

She was more than an hour off course and much further south than she needed to be. She could stay on her current route, link back up with I-40 near the Arkansas border but that'd have her pulling into Nashville around six in the morning.

Nashville. Home.

The thought of returning to her childhood home, to her mother, filled her with an uncomfortable mix of discomfort, shame, regret, anger, and, paradoxically, safety and longing.

She didn't *want* to go home, but she *needed* to. She'd been gone three long years, with only a few brief visits since she'd left. Amarillo had everything she wanted, the lifestyle, the atmosphere, the funky art, hell, even the food. Perhaps most importantly, it was a long, long drive from Tennessee.

It also had Texas A&M, where until the middle of this semester Helen had been a student. She began her time there as a bright-eyed, seemingly well-adjusted daughter of the odd overlapping area where the South met the Midwest.

5

A strong, confident young woman had arrived on campus with a full ride scholarship, only to slowly implode over the course of three years until she'd arrived at her current state – failing all but one of her classes, deep in student loan debt, and with her mental and emotional health hurtling towards rock bottom.

And, of course, running back home to mommy with her tail tucked between her legs.

Helen fought back tears of frustration, tossed her phone into the passenger seat, and laid her forehead against the steering wheel. Gravity pulled her wild, tawny curls into a mane around her face as she focused on trying to regulate her emotions.

She could picture her mother now, meticulously arranging things in the same ways and places she had since Helen was a child, carefully avoiding any direct discussion of Helen's latest failure.

"Of course you can stay as long as you'd like," she'd say. "It's your home too, after all!"

"That Texan heat is awful anyway," she'd say and pat Helen awkwardly on the shoulder. "You didn't really belong there."

"Turn left, then turn left."

Helen reached over and tapped the screen.

"Recalculating... We've found a faster route. Would you like to-"

"Enough, already!" Helen leaned over, grabbed her phone, and began mashing at the screen until the tiny, obnoxious voice was silenced at last.

She dropped the phone into her lap and tried to resist the urge to punch something. Instead she straightened her back and closed her eyes, taking a deep breath. As she moved, her phone slipped between her legs and onto the floor by the pedals.

Helen grit her teeth hard enough to send shooting pain up into her jaw, exhaled slowly, and bent swiftly to recover the device. In her haste, she bounced her forehead off the steering wheel, letting off a loud blast of the horn and leaving her with a rapidly fading red mark.

Her attempts to maintain a calm demeanor finally failed. She grabbed the steering wheel on both sides, yanking at it with enough force to shake the small car, and screamed a string of expletives that would make a seasoned sailor blush. She ended her tirade by punching the center console with enough force to jam one of the buttons in.

"Damn it!" she shouted, rubbing her bruised knuckles before retrieving her phone more carefully. "I just want to-"

A loud bang above her stopped her mid-sentence. It *sounded* like something had hit the roof of the car. She unclipped her seatbelt and scooted back to squint up through the sunroof just in time to see another rock, this one about the size of a baseball, fall from the darkness of the cliff wall above and bounce off the glass. The impact sent a spider web of cracks across the pane and she flinched instinctively.

Helen shifted back to the driver's seat, suddenly feeling the car start to wobble back and forth, the ground crumbling away under her tires as she tried to secure her seat. Looking out through the windshield, she could see that the car was now sitting sideways on an angle downward, towards the river.

"Shit," she turned the keys in the ignition and listened to the aging motor sputter and gasp. "Shit-shit-shit."

The vehicle roared to life at last, and she threw it in drive with the gas pedal to the floor. But she was too late. Gravel flew and tires spun uselessly as the ground beneath her gave way, sending the vehicle tumbling downward.

Two terrifying seconds of near-weightlessness stretched into infinity as Helen's mind scrambled to react to the landslide. Moments later, her car hit the water, a shower of rocks raining down on her as cold, dark water enveloped her.

The steering-wheel airbag hit her in the face like a boxing glove and she felt her jaw pop. The impact stunned her and, for a moment, she couldn't even tell which direction was up. She blinked a few times, struggling to hold onto consciousness as the vehicle lurched back and forth. Her vision was blurring, and her surroundings were starting to lose color and clarity. She could tell the vehicle was filling with water, and every now and then they would hit something and she'd once again be painfully tossed about.

Helen's heart was racing, her hands shaking, and her brain too foggy to cling to anything but the realization that she needed to get out, *somehow* she needed to get out of this car. She reached for the door handle beside her and started to push the door open. The force of the water pushing against it made her effort nearly useless.

With all of her concentration on the door, she missed an approaching rocky outcropping.

The car slammed into it with all the force of a highway wreck and Helen felt her wrist bend painfully back until something snapped. In a fraction of a second, her head and shoulder slammed against the dashboard and then rebounded against the glass of the side window. As her face bounced off the glass, she felt a crack just under her left eye and slipped into an all-consuming darkness.

Helen sat up with a short, sharp scream, instinctively thrashing around as her mind struggled to reorient itself. Within seconds, she was breathing hard and struggling in vain, tangled hopelessly in... blankets?

Her eyes wide, she scanned her surroundings and her confusion mounted as she detangled herself. She was in a bed - a rather large one at that - topped with soft white linens. The bed was the dominant feature of a spacious bedroom equipped with worn wooden furnishings, immaculate hardwood floors, and the kind of cream-colored plaster walls that you only found in really old homes. The most modern feature in the room was the addition of electric wall sconces, and even they looked decades old. The soft, warm light they gave off did its best to drown out the crushing darkness of the still-raging storm outside the windows of the bedroom.

Peering out the window, Helen jumped at the sudden, violent flash and bang of a thunder-and-lightning combo that shook the glass in the panes.

She forced herself to take slow, even breaths as she reached for a familiar grounding exercise Abigail had taught her a few years ago.

She started by counting five things she could see - the bed, the window, the lamp, the dresser, and the door. Next up, four that she could hear - the rain, her own breathing, the soft electric hum of the lights, and the whine of the winds. On and on she continued through her senses. The last thing she needed was to add a dissociative episode to her bizarre situation. Her train of thought trailed off as she narrowed her eyes and examined things even more closely.

Oh, God, *was* she having an episode?

The calm she had restored within herself frayed by the second as she worked through her mental state as best as she could. Feeling closer and closer to the edge, she cast around for a less healthy

- but more effective - method of re-establishing control. From where she was sitting in the bed, she reached a hand up to the nearest wall sconce - helpfully situated as a nearby reading light - and wrapped her fingers around the glass bulb.

Pain shot through her palm and fingers instantly as she touched the hot glass and she recoiled with a relieved sigh. In her experience so far, pain had always meant she was, in fact, lucid. The pain in her hand triggered the floodgates for the rest of her body which had - whether due to adrenaline or some other factor - remained relatively quiet in the moments since she'd woken up. Now, however, she felt like an apple that had been rolled down a staircase. Bruised muscles and battered bones competed with a headache of epic proportions, and her recent struggle with the sheets left her feeling all around ill-used. She lifted her hands to touch her face, wincing at the sparks of pain along her jaw and around her eye.

Shouldn't you be dead?

Helen sat back against the headboard, cradling her hand and considering her situation, and was hit by another realization. She wasn't wearing the clothes she'd been driving in.

She kicked off the blanket to examine herself and found that she was wearing a faded flannel pajama set - a pullover shirt and full length trousers - in checkered black and green.

While she was grateful to not be wearing soaking wet clothes - or to be dead at the bottom of the river - she wasn't sure how comfortable she was with her mysterious benefactor having changed her clothes while she was unconscious. Of course, she'd yet to really address the fact that *someone* had brought her... wherever she was. She wasn't dead, bound, or in a cage, so she supposed whoever it was mustn't mean her immediate harm.

After briefly considering staying where she was and waiting to see what happened, she swung her feet off the edge of the bed and gingerly tried to stand. Her right ankle, knee, and hip protested but held her weight and she was able to hobble to the door without incident.

Her bare feet were silent against the warm grain of the floors, and not a single board so much as squeaked at her passing. The door handle was a heavy, silver affair that turned with a soft click, releasing a smooth and silent door that swung open to reveal a long, straight hallway with doors on either side.

Helen tread cautiously into the hall, torn between trying the handles she passed and pushing onward to the end of the hall. She was curious, of course, but not to the extent that she wanted to find her host - not before locating an exit, just in case.

The hall terminated in a squarish sort of landing, and her eyes were drawn instantly to the massive gray marble spiral staircase that filled one side of the space. It was exquisite, every line and curve crafted to such smoothness that the entire structure flowed like water from above, through the level she stood upon, and then down to a lower level. The railings on either side were carved to resemble flowering rose vines, and the sculptor had even taken the time to carve fallen leaves and petals into the edges of every step.

Helen noted the rest of the landing in her peripheral vision - one wall featured another hallway extending off perpendicular to the one she'd just occupied, and the another wall simply held a broad wooden double-door - but she could not help but be drawn to the stairs.

The stone called to her. It stirred something in her blood and pulled her across the hardwood until she was at last close enough to reach out a trembling hand to the rail. It was icy, cool, and smooth as glass, and the second her skin made contact she felt a sort of... *electricity* flowing through her, like the static before a lightning strike. Rather than lessen, the pull from the staircase upon her heart intensified, and she felt her gaze pulled upward.

The next level up was dark, and she couldn't make out much detail from her place at the edge of the stair, so she stepped forward, craning her neck up and around, searching the shadows above for any hint of what might be hidden there.

"I *should* go down," she muttered to herself, shaking her head and willing her feet to respond. "Down and more importantly *out-*."

A clatter, as if of pots and pans banging together, shook her from her trance and had her crouching instinctively in the shadows. It was the first unnatural sound she'd heard since waking, and it had undeniably come from downstairs.

"H-hello?" she squeaked, eyes wide and ears straining.

Her barely audible question went unanswered and eventually her curiosity got the better of her. She re-crossed the landing and peered downward instead. It was, in stark contrast to the path upward, well lit and inviting.

She felt herself torn between the presumed safety of the bedroom down the hall, the intoxicating mystery of the darkened path above, and the more obvious - if intimidating - trek down the winding stairs toward the only sign of life she'd heard yet.

Ultimately, it was her nose that made the decision. A draft from down below brought up with it two of the most heart-warming and unmistakable scents known to mankind - fresh coffee and sizzling bacon.

Tip-toeing down the stairs, she moved silently across the winding marble until she hit the ground floor some twelve feet below. Unlike the smooth wood of the second floor, the staircase let out into a wide room with matching marble tiles of alternating rose and off-white cream.

The parlor itself had several posh but older looking couches, a chaise, a broad coffee table made of some dark, tight-grained wood, and a number of chairs that practically begged for smoking jackets and cigars. The walls of the room had a dark wood wainscotting under creamy, textured plaster walls, inset all the way around with deep shelves filled to the brim with books large and small. Two of the other walls featured broad archways, more than wide enough for three to walk abreast and arcing up nearly to the ceiling.

The entire place reminded her of a television set - some inexplicable combination of a foreboding gothic mansion and a warm, inviting museum.

She wandered close to the bookshelves as she made her way across the room. On her way, she noted that some of the tiles, specifically those closest to the center, were engraved to look like chess pieces deeply embroiled in a complex match. Helen was a former champion at the state and regional levels, as well as a formerly respected competitor at nationals, and to her trained eyes the layout was not some random hodge-podge but a stellar representation of two masters hard at work.

As captivating as the floor was, and as unusual as the scene, it was the bizarre and senseless arrangement of the books against the walls that most threw her for a loop. They were shelved in what appeared to be the furthest possible method from alphabetization by either author or title. Some books were literally upside down or even backwards, presenting the bare edge of their pages rather than the spine. They weren't arranged by topic either, as far as she could tell. Autobiographies rubbed shoulders with fiction, textbooks with memoirs, and with all manner of oddity in between.

"Ahem."

The soft, delicate cough behind her had Helen nearly jumping out of her skin. She spun around to see a short, immaculately dressed man staring at her expectantly. The fellow was perhaps five-two, and very young of face. His high cheekbones and flat brown eyes lent him an unnerving, doll-like quality that was further enhanced by his pristine, 1920's style butler uniform.

"Shall I convey you to the kitchen, madam?"

"I, err, what?"

The man's voice was soft, delicate even, but clear, further throwing her off balance.

"Breakfast will be served momentarily. If it pleases, I can direct you."

"O-okay," she stuttered.

The young man bowed at the waist and then silently turned and walked towards the nearer of the two archways.

"Wait, um…" she tagged along cautiously. "What's your name? I'm-"

"The dining hall is this way."

Helen's mouth snapped shut. She knew a dismissal when she heard one.

They spent the next few moments walking in uncomfortable silence. Thankfully, the hall was short, and only a few doors dotted the sides as they made their way to a double door at the end. These doors were broad and wooden and stout, so Helen was more than a little surprised when her petite companion pushed them aside with a silent ease. The doors swung wide and he stepped out of the way, bowed, and waited with a hand out toward the empty dining room beyond.

The dining room, it was more of a hall, was dominated by a large, smooth, wooden banquet table that looked like it could seat around twenty. It was, however, set only for two; the head of the table and the place directly to its right.

Wide flower arrangements - all composed entirely of roses - filled the centerline of the table, and accented the walls of the room as well, which featured more of the dark wood and plaster, and were bedecked with a variety of paintings large and small.

"Should I-?"

"You may take your seat, madam," the man cut her off, inclining his head to the far end of the table where two place settings lay.

Helen followed his gaze, noting that the only other entrance to the large room was a small servant door at the back corner.

"Which one do I-," she turned back to the man but found him gone and the large doors tightly shut once again, "-use..." she finished lamely and to no one in particular.

Helen groaned and made her way down the table, admiring the craftsmanship and the overall elegance of the room as she went. The place settings were intimidating, with a full set of forks, bowls, plates, and spoons. She had some basic knowledge of etiquette thanks to her Oma, the all-knowing matriarch of her family, but nothing that would prepare her for this.

She'd just reached the head of the table when the servants' door opened and a woman entered, balancing two large platters in her hands. The woman came through backwards, opening the door with her rear end; she was wearing a modest-but-comfortable dress with an apron tied on. Helen caught sight of bare feet and bare legs from the knee down as the woman spun, deftly avoiding Helen and sliding the dishes onto the table with a wink and a flash of a brilliant white smile that stopped Helen's heart.

She was a bronze-skinned goddess, all of six-foot and with fierce black curls and mercurial golden-brown eyes. Below the shoulder of her dress were unapologetically strong arms with smooth, rippling muscle, and her heartshaped face caught

Helen's attention with such a tightness that she forgot for a moment how to breathe.

"How are you feeling?"

It took all of Helen's brainpower to form an answer.

"I-I'm alright," she managed, rubbing her wrist. "Better than I ought to be, I think."

Miraculously.

"Nothing broken?"

Helen shook her head, but couldn't meet the woman's intense eyes. She looked down nervously, fixating on the chairs in front of her.

"You can sit at either," the woman's voice was warm, soft, and sweet like fresh-baked cookies.

Helen couldn't compose herself enough to speak, and so her mouth worked soundlessly for a moment as the newcomer divided up plates of thinly sliced ham and cheeses, pastries, breads, fruits, and something that looked like tortillas covered in salsa or pico de gallo.

"But what if-"

"Don't worry," the woman's accent was as mesmerizing as her smile was mischievous. "Your host won't mind either way."

Helen managed a weak smile, but she was still too dazzled to make much sense of her own thoughts.

"Suit yourself," the woman turned and headed back to the servant door, which Helen now suspected led to a kitchen.

"Wait!"

She stopped and turned expectantly.

Oh, fuck, why did I say that?

"I…" Helen panicked. "I didn't catch your name or the name of that other guy…"

The woman paused, both of the now-empty platters under one arm, and brushed some invisible speck of dirt from her apron.

"I'm Luciana, and his name is Armand."

Helen opened her mouth to say more, but Luciana had already disappeared through the dark wood of the six-panel door.

Her cheeks still flushed a rosy pink, she turned back to the table. She felt awkward choosing the seat at the head of the table, so she stepped around to the side and slid out the heavy wooden chair at the second place setting. She took her seat and waited as patiently as she could, taking note of the unusual spread and feeling totally out of place in her flannel pajamas.

"Sorry for that," Luciana's soft, lightly accented voice called out from behind her a few minutes later. "I like to get hands-on in the kitchen, especially when we have guests."

Helen turned and tried not to show her surprise. She felt her eyes widen and her jaw threatened to pop open as Luciana, now clad in a form-fitting scarlet sundress with a cream-and-gold flower pattern along the hem, stepped back into the room. She sported twin sets of gold hoop earrings and a simple golden necklace, but her golden eyes continued to be the centerpiece that took Helen's breath away.

"Welcome to Casa de Rosas."

Chapter Two

"This is *your* house?"

"I live here, yes," Luciana replied with a gentle, tinkling laugh. "Though I am not the original architect. This property is quite old."

"It's beautiful," Helen managed to squeak out, reaching for a glass of water to quench her sudden thirst.

"Thank you. Armand does a magnificent job of helping me keep it… running smoothly," Luciana gave a small nod. "We share the sentiment that this place deserves to be cared for."

Helen tried not to stare, fascinated by the delicate movements of the woman's supple fingers as she cut fresh strawberries and brought them bite by bite to her full, pouty lips.

Luciana caught her staring and paused mid-bite. Her mouth turned up in a crooked half smile as Helen's face all but burst into flames.

"Problem?"

"No," Helen squeaked. "N-no, I, um, I was just wondering how exactly I got here? What... What exactly happened?"

Luciana's eyes clouded unexpectedly and she turned her attention back to her plate of food with a sudden distance.

"I'm guessing your car crashed into the river," she began after a moment's pause. "I'm not sure how far upstream, but you floated down far enough to hit our bridge."

Helen blanched, flashes of unwelcome imagery entering her mind.

"Your car hit it hard enough to destroy it, and it got lodged against some rocks in the process," Luciana continued. "With Armand's help, I was able to climb down and pull you out. You're fortunate to be alive."

"You saved my life," Helen's eyes were wide with shock. "I... I don't know what I could ever-"

"Ah-ta-ta," Luciana tutted at her, raising a hand and shaking her head. "There is no debt."

"There is no debt..." Helen repeated slowly, stumbling over the phrasing. "Well-"

"Correct."

That was odd.

A moment passed in awkward silence, the room still and quiet save for the soft clink and scrape of their utensils. The food was exquisite. Even the unfamiliar tortilla dish was flavorful, spicy, and refreshing.

"Oh my god," Helen realized aloud. "I *destroyed your bridge?*"

"You did," Luciana laughed. "Quite thoroughly in fact. It'll likely be several days before anyone from the outside world can come out and repair it too, let alone retrieve your car."

"So, hang on, we're stuck here?"

"Well, *stuck* makes it sound like you're not a fan of the place," Luciana cracked another smile. "But, sadly, until the bridge is repaired, there's no road leaving the estate."

"I'm sorry, I didn't mean it like that-"

"Helen," Luciana smiled, a brilliant flash of white against her tan skin and dark lips. "I'm only teasing."

Something about the way the woman said her name made Helen feel squishy and warm, but not so much so that she forgot herself entirely.

"Ah, shit," Helen groaned as her mind and memory continued to awaken. "I need to call my mom, she'll be freaking out right about now. I suppose my cellphone is ruined?"

"It *was* damaged in the crash, I'm afraid," Luciana frowned as crookedly - and enchantingly - as she'd smiled before. "So I optimistically put it in a bowl of rice in the kitchen. But we do have a landline that you're welcome to use in the meantime."

"Thanks," Helen pushed back from the table then stopped herself. "I'm sorry, d'you mind if I do that now? I don't mean to be rude."

"Not at all," her host stood as well. "Let me show you the way."

Luciana seemed content to leave her dishes on the table as she stepped lightly away, so Helen resisted her deeply ingrained temptation to offer to help with the clean-up. Instead, she followed a few steps behind Luciana and took the opportunity to get a clearer look at the woman. She was taller than Helen by a good six inches. She was athletic, but not what Helen would describe as thin; rather she had a volleyball player's build - strong, tall, and substantial.

The woman moved with the grace of a dancer though, and every action she took looked effortless and smooth. She led the way to a parlor, or maybe it would be better described as an office. Several leather chairs sat at a tall, imposing, wooden desk in the center of the room. Bookshelves and various antiquities completed the space, tying together an expensive rug and the maps and charts hanging from the walls.

There was no computer, no laptop or tablet, or other modern convenience at the desk. Instead, there was a shiny black and brass typewriter and an ancient looking rotary phone.

"Take your time," Luciana smiled, setting a hand on Helen's shoulder and giving her a gentle squeeze.

Helen was too flustered to respond with more than a nod and a shaky smile as her host turned and left the room again, closing the door with a soft click.

Helen's beet-red face, now hidden from view, turned to an expression usually reserved for gushing fans at concerts. She collapsed heavily into the leather swivel-chair behind the desk and laid her head down on the desk.

"Alright," she shook herself back to the task at hand. "Alright, you can do this."

But despite her self-assurance, she found her left hand hovering over the receiver, unable to pick it up.

Her mother was... imposing, and the circumstances of her return were already embarrassing and shameful. Even so, the damage was done and the band-aid might as well get ripped off all at once.

She drew a sharp breath, and with her off-hand she flipped the worn brass ring of the rotary, dialing the old familiar number of her childhood home.

The phone rang three times before, just as Helen expected it to go to voicemail, she heard a metallic click.

"LeFitte residence, this is Janice."

"Hey, Mom, it's-"

"Helen," her mother's tone was one of annoyance, *"I assume there's a reason you didn't come home last night?"*

"Yeah, mom, I was-"

"It's terribly rude, you know, having someone wait up and worry about you. I didn't know if anything had happened to you, God knows what!"

"Yes, mom, that's what I'm trying to say. I-"

"Well, of course it's behind us now, no apology needed I suppose," another huffy sigh. *"What time should I actually expect-"*

"I was in a car wreck, mom," Helen finally blurted out.

Deafening silence.

"Were you drinking or anything? Are you in any trouble?"

"Jesus, mom, no!"

"Well am I to assume you're alright, at least?"

"I'm… fine. Look, it's gonna be a few days 'til I can get out of here. Sorry."

"I suppose."

"You suppose?"

"Helen, if you're just not coming home, you don't have to make up a story."

"Mom," every word forced past clenched teeth, "I was literally *in a car wreck.* I totaled my car and could have died."

"Alright, Helen, it's just you don't sound like you've been in a car wreck, that's all."

It was Helen's turn to fall silent.

"Are you still there?"

"Yes."

"Well, you're not saying anything."

"What am I supposed to say?"

"Where are you, a hotel?"

Helen balked, uncertain suddenly how truthful she should be.

"Uh, I'm in Oklahoma."

Her mother waited a beat before answering.

"Precision, Helen," she snipped. *"Where are you?"*

"I'm... I'm staying with a friend outside of Oklahoma City."

"Who on earth do you know in-"

"Look, I've... got to run, mom," she ran her free hand through her hair. "I'm fine. I'll call you ... uh... soon."

She replaced the receiver with a sharp click and rubbed her temples. Speaking with her mother always caused her anxiety to spike. Already she could feel the pounding of her own heart and feel her chest starting to tighten. Next she began to feel the tell-tale lump in her throat that always precipitated a panic attack.

Helen's veins ran cold as she realized that all of her medication was at the bottom of the river and that there was no chance she'd have any of it for days.

"Fuck."

She closed her eyes tightly, willing herself to breathe through it. She was deep in concentration when a soft tapping at the door caused her to look up with a start.

"Helen?"

Luciana's soft voice was muffled but unmistakable through the heavy door.

"I'm taking coffee in the library," she continued. "Take your time. I'll make sure Armand makes enough for you as well."

Luciana looked surprised when, a moment later, Helen pulled the door open.

"Done already?"

"Mhmm," Helen forced herself to smile.

Something in Luciana's eyes gave Helen pause. There was a wisdom there, an understanding beyond her age that Helen hadn't expected to see.

"I understand," her host nodded. "In that case, you're welcome to accompany me."

Helen nodded her acceptance and followed the other woman back through the halls of the house until they reached the library at the base of the stairs. Armand was already there, waiting beside a porcelain tray that held tea and coffee for two.

"I wasn't sure if you drink coffee," Luciana admitted with a shrug. "So I had Armand prepare tea, as well. We keep some on hand, though I don't really drink it often."

"Coffee would be great." Helen sniffed the air, the bold rich aroma of the carafe on the tray was mesmerizing. It was certainly coffee, as promised, but it had an earthiness to it, a smooth strength that bespoke quality.

She took one of the seats around a coffee table off to the side of the room and was pleasantly surprised by the squishy comfort of the high-backed leather chair. Luciana took a seat opposite her, in the middle of a finely upholstered chaise lounge chair. The deep, almost black purple of the upholstery played well with the extremely dark wood of the piece, and both set off the warm tones in Luciana's dress as well as her soft brown skin.

Helen waited awkwardly as Armand poured her a cup of coffee.

"Cream or sugar, ma'am?"

Helen shook her head no, smiled gratefully, and reached for the delicate saucer and cup that the man handed her.

Luciana also took her coffee black, and as soon as her beverage was poured, Armand took a deep bow and left the two of them alone once more.

Silence filled the library as the two sipped their coffee. Helen was stunned at the taste of it and was certain that this single cup of coffee would ruin her for the rest of her life. She nearly asked Luciana where she'd gotten it, but dismissed the question before it left her lips.

"So," Luciana broke the silence at last, "what had you braving such a storm anyway, Helen?"

A loud crackling boom of thunder accentuated her question, echoing through the unseen halls before fading into the stone.

"I was headed home actually," she took another sip. "Back to Tennessee."

"Home?"

"Yeah, Knoxville. I lived… uh, *live* there with my mom."

Luciana raised an eyebrow but changed the subject.

"So a trip brought you through Oklahoma then. Business or pleasure?"

"N-neither," Helen found herself flustered by something in the way Luciana phrased the question. "I was heading home from school."

"Interesting."

"Interesting?"

"Well, it isn't spring break, it isn't a *holiday*," Luciana stirred her coffee, her eyes downcast and seemingly focused entirely on the cup. "It isn't even the weekend…"

"Ah, right."

"Sorry, I don't mean to pry."

"No, it… it's a fair question." Helen searched for words, something that wouldn't make her failure so apparent, but came up empty-handed. "I'm, uh, I'm dropping out," she shrugged defeatedly.

Luciana's silence gnawed at her.

"I had been doing so well," she blurted out. "Things sort of just fell apart, I guess?"

Luciana nodded, safely taking a sip of her coffee before looking Helen in the eyes. Her gaze was utterly devoid of judgment; rather, she appeared content to listen quietly.

"I don't really know what happened," Helen was unusually emboldened by her captive listener. "Things *started* well enough. I had a full ride. A *full ride* to Texas A&M!"

She stood, suddenly too restless for her chair. She turned away, reexamining the vast bookcases and the cool, checkered floor.

"I don't know what's wrong with me," she hung her head. "I stopped showing up for classes.

I've spent more time drinking than studying, even when I didn't *want* to."

Helen's hands tightened until the coffee cup shook between her clenched fingers.

"I had a shot. I had a chance to get the hell out, and I threw it away. I fell to pieces and nothing I do seems to ever-" Helen paused and took a slow, calming breath, unwilling to allow the pent up frustration and guilt within herself to bubble forth - not when her host had treated her so graciously.

With her best smile, she turned back to Luciana and took a deliberate sip of her coffee, "I'm sorry. I'm still a bit... stressed, I think."

"No apology needed," Luciana waved. "I'm sorry for interrogating you after such a traumatic event. I should be the one apologizing."

Helen stared at the floor a while, unable or unwilling to look Luciana in the face, until she heard her host take a few slow steps closer.

"How about a tour?"

She breathed a sigh of relief and nodded, still cupping her coffee and standing, awkwardly facing her host.

Luciana led the way through the first floor of the house. It wasn't quite as expansive as Helen had first believed but it still took the rest of the morning to get through all of the elaborately tiled bathrooms, opulent but tasteful studies, gorgeous workspaces, and finally, the understated but exquisite gallery.

Helen couldn't help but gasp as they entered this last room. The space was easily forty feet wide, with high vaulted ceilings and bright, clear lighting thanks to well-spaced globe lights placed along the wall. Paintings lined the walls almost from floor to ceiling, and the entire center of the hall was filled with sculptures.

"It's magnificent," she mumbled, spinning on a slow circle. "It's like your own private museum!"

The more she looked, the more she fell in love. The hall had to be one hundred feet or more, and she realized it must be the wing under the hallway that held her bedroom. The paintings, at this end, were all in cool colors - lots of blues and whites and winter scenes, and it seemed that, as the gallery extended outward, the color palette did indeed follow the turning of the seasons. The cold winter giving way through muted browns to the vibrant green and popping colors of spring. Then, the warm golds of summer, and the equally stunning reds, oranges, and browns of autumn. It was superbly arranged and flowed seamlessly from end to end. The artwork on the walls alone would've been the crowning jewel of any museum, but the statuary down the center was the sort of art that stirred the very soul.

The first piece she came upon was a life-size statue of a woman. She had her arms at her sides and her hair was stirred as if by a soft breeze; she was wearing a sheer dress that clung to her as though she were standing in the rain. Every line and curve in the stone was rendered in perfect detail, so much so that Helen half expected the thing to start moving.

"The artist named this one 'Lydia,'" Luciana added helpfully.

"Who *is* the artist?" Helen breathed. "Surely one of the greats?"

"An excellent question," Luciana shrugged. "Their work only exists here though, in this estate."

"*Here*? In the middle-of-nowhere Oklahoma?"

"I suppose that no one knows why that is either," the woman sighed, running slender fingers across the stone. "But I'm glad to share the company of these precious creations."

"Do you not, you know, *go out*?"

Luciana looked back with a surprised smirk.

"Oh my gosh that was so rude," Helen gasped, her hands flying to her mouth. "I'm so sorry, I didn't mean that-"

Smooth.

"No, no," Luciana laughed. "You're quite alright. It's true, I don't get out much. I haven't left for... quite some time."

"But don't you miss it, the outside world?"

"Would you believe me if I said no?"

Helen realized that somehow, she would indeed. There was a melancholy in Luciana's eyes as she turned back to the artwork that kept Helen from pressing further.

"Helen, I've seen a lot of the outside world," the woman turned to one of the paintings - a bleak depiction of a foggy winter forest. "Much of what I found was beautiful, inspiring, wondrous. But - for me at least - there is a great deal of pain out there. Pain I would prefer not to revisit."

"You sound like me," Helen chuckled dryly. "Prematurely soured on the world at large."

"Prematurely?"

"Well, I just meant that, y'know," Helen's cheeks brightened again. "Well, you're *young*, that's all. You can't be more than a few years older than - what's so funny?"

Luciana was laughing brightly, her eyes alight and her smile wide and carefree.

"And how old do you think I am?"

"Uh," Helen looked down at the floor and scuffed her shoe. "Twenty... eight? Maybe thirty?"

"Well, let's just call it 'something like that,' shall we?" Luciana winked conspiratorially.

Helen hid the red in her cheeks by turning back to the artwork. She stepped closer to an Autumn scene and studiously examined the many intricate leaves on each tree.

"Well how old is all of this then?" she gestured broadly. "Surely that's less... secret?"

"Oh, it's hard to say really," Luciana stepped closer, now standing just a few feet behind her guest. "I'd wager it's quite old though, maybe a century or two?"

"Two hundred years," Helen exclaimed, turning and finding that Luciana was closer than she'd thought. "D-do you really think so?"

"Mhmm," she nodded, her hands behind her back and her roguish smile gracing her lips once more.

Luciana stepped brightly away, headed back the way they'd come.

"We're leaving?"

"You don't *have* to," she looked back. "But don't you want to see the rest of the house too?"

"It's just, it's all so beautiful."

"Well, I doubt this storm will let up any time soon so you should have plenty of time," she smiled as she reached a hand out toward Helen. "Besides, as long as you're here, you're welcome to spend as much time admiring the artwork as you like, I promise."

"I'll hold you to that," Helen found the woman's smile infectious and was quickly grinning as well.

They backtracked through the parts of the house Helen had already seen. Luciana kept up a thoughtful and informative commentary on noteworthy features - explaining the significance of this mural or that particular archway - while Helen did her best to follow along.

It wasn't that the explanations weren't interesting, they certainly were, but the soft flow of Luciana's dress, the way her short curls bounced with such energy, worked relentlessly to capture her attention over and over. When Luciana finally let go of her hand, it felt suddenly devoid of warmth, and she had to fight the urge to frown.

"Everything alright?"

"What?" Helen blinked, a deer caught in the proverbial headlights. "Oh yes, sorry. I'm good, er, great thank you!"

She took a quick glance around, somehow they'd made it all the way back to the large winding staircase.

Helen shook her head, clearing it momentarily of the fog that built every second she spent in Luciana's company.

"Did you want to see the upstairs now? Or perhaps lie down or…?"

"Uh, well now that you mention it," Helen shrugged apologetically. "I'm still pretty exhausted. I don't know how I made it out of that wreck without… well without being worse off and I think my body is still in shock."

"I'm very glad you *did* make it out."

Luciana stepped up and put her hands on Helen's shoulders. At this closeness their difference in height was quite noticeable and Helen found herself looking up at the chiseled jawline and bright eyes of her host.

"Now, get some rest."

Helen smiled broadly, but couldn't get her tongue to work properly so she simply nodded and turned toward the stairs.

As soon as she was around the corner and out of sight, she let go of the breath she hadn't realized she was holding in. She felt like a helium balloon, like she was floating off the marble stair. Instantly, her face was covered in a sappy giddy smile and she was nearly skipping by the time she reached the landing.

She turned at once to head toward her room, but found herself pausing just a few steps later.

The *tug* of the upstairs gripped her once more and she slowly circled back around.

"A quick peek won't hurt," she muttered, stepping forward and reaching for the railing.

Her foot scarcely hit the first stair upwards when she felt a presence behind her.

"Helen?"

She squeaked and spun around, guilt turning her cheeks bright pink.

"I forgot to mention."

Luciana's voice was still sweet, but there was a steely undertone to it now. How she'd managed to appear silently just a few steps behind Helen was a mystery, but there she was nonetheless.

"I would prefer that you not go upstairs," she cocked her head ever so slightly to the side. "The third floor is, well it's a… private work space. I'm sure you understand?"

"Y-yes of course," Helen gulped, fighting the urge to take a step back. "Not a problem at all."

Two heartbeats of silence passed before Luciana broke out into a wide smile again.

"Great! I'll send Armand around for dinner."

"Thank you, Luciana," she resisted a peculiar urge to bow. "For everything."

She turned toward her bedroom and didn't look back until the door was shut firmly behind her.

Helen crossed the room quickly and slumped down on the bed, sighing deeply.

"That was weird, right?"

She stood again, too restless to be still.

"No, I was being nosey," she began to pace. "Why shouldn't she want some privacy, it's *her* house."

She wrestled with herself for what felt like ages, wearing out the floorboards as she paced back and forth. Nothing about her interactions with her host had been out of the ordinary, but she couldn't shake the feeling that something was off.

Finally she worried herself into exhaustion, and the building weight of the trauma she'd undergone the day before began to slow her footsteps.

More and more often her inner dialogue was punctuated with wide, jaw-popping yawns and she found herself yearning to lie down.

"Just for a moment," she reassured herself as she reclined atop the comforter on the newly-made bed.

Chapter Three

She fought valiantly against the tug of reality, but eventually gave in to the idea that she was, in fact, awake.

She sat up slowly, pushing through the tangled nest of blankets and sheets she'd built around herself, as her brain stumbled into wakefulness. It took her a moment to remember exactly why she was waking up in a strange bed, and the circumstances of the morning.

Her stomach growled as she rubbed the sleep from her eyes, and she realized she had no idea what time it was.

Her ears told her that the storm was still raging outside, so the darkness in the windows did little to help her determine just how spectacularly she might've overslept.

Helen slipped her glasses on after retrieving them from beside the bed, allowing the world to come into better focus as she reluctantly committed to joining the waking world.

Late or not, her stomach wouldn't be ignored so she crept from the bed and let out a long, slow, whole-body stretch. She felt her shoulders and neck crack, and was pleased to find she was a little less tender and bruised.

Helen paused mid-stretch as she noticed something on the floor in front of the door - a piece of paper was laying there face down.

She walked over and bent to retrieve it, surprised at the weight and feel of the item. It wasn't the standard printer paper she was used to. It felt rough and thick beneath her fingertips

"What is this, parchment?"

She yawned as she turned the page over to reveal flowing, immaculate cursive.

Helen,

I knocked (softly) but you were still asleep. You looked so peaceful I didn't want to wake you up.

There's a plate of fruit on the nightstand-

Helen glanced up, surprised she'd missed it, but sure enough there was a covered silver plate beside the bed.

If you want something more substantial there's risotto in the oven downstairs. It's on warm, so be careful. Help yourself to anything else down there and please make yourself at home.

Affectionately yours,

Luciana De La Rosa

Helen found herself smiling as she walked back to the edge of the bed and sat down. She placed the letter on the nightstand and lifted the cover of the tray to reveal a collection of grapes, kiwis, oranges, apples, and other fruit. There were also candied almonds and pecans, as well as a croissant, and a little dish that held butter and jam.

She let out a low whistle upon seeing the spread, her stomach rumbling in agreement.

"Well," she mumbled, selecting a plump green grape and popping it into her mouth, "you sure set the bar high for a midnight snack."

Helen dug in. Each element of the dish was better than the last. The croissant crackled wonderfully as she bit into it, the flaky layers complimenting the tart, sticky sweetness of the raspberry jam and the cool, creamy butter. The fruit was all perfectly ripe, crisp, and sweet. Even the candied nuts were the ideal blend of sweet, crunchy, and savory.

She pushed the tray away some time later, the edge now gone from her hunger. There was plenty left on the dish but she'd had her fill of the lighter fare. What she really wanted was something more substantial.

Besides, she should apologize for missing lunch at least.

The hallway was darker than it had been. Each of the wall lights now emitted only a dim glow - enough to see by, but not in much detail. Helen worried that perhaps she'd missed more than lunch. Certainly she couldn't have slept the whole day, all the way through dinner?

Helen made her way down the hallway towards the stairs more confidently than she had earlier in the day. Her steps were sure and relaxed as she traversed the hardwood.

Until she heard the drums.

It was impossible to tell when she first became aware of the deep, rhythmic sound, but she froze mid-step when she realized that the noise was real and not simply in her head.

It was slow, low, and persistent, a distant pounding that - now that she was aware of it - could be felt in the floor, the air, and in her very blood. It was coming from further down the hall, and as she continued toward the stairway, she realized it was in fact coming from upstairs.

It sounded simultaneously distant and crystal clear, both entrancing and in some ways menacing. Should she risk the ill will of her host and investigate, or let it be? Helen wrestled with herself as she drew near, unsure which path she would choose.

The choice was taken from her though. The moment she stepped onto the marble landing the drums ceased. Instant silence fell, accompanied by a flash of dark red light from around the curve of the spiral staircase.

The intense burst illuminated the stairs and even much of the hallway behind her, but only for a moment. Helen waited, expecting something to come of the bizarre occurrence, but was met with innocent, unassuming silence and the dim, steady lighting of the hallway fixtures.

Moments passed and still nothing untoward appeared. No more drums, no more tremors or flashes of light. Only the growing fear that none of it had really happened at all.

Of course it didn't happen, you're crazy.

Shut up.

Tick-tock, how long before you snap?

"Hello," she blurted out finally, unable to keep her peace. "Is anyone there?"

Silence.

Obviously.

Her stomach waged a war with her doubts, each vying to gnaw at her more deeply. Her stomach won, if only because it was aided by her curiosity.

She made her way quickly back down the stairs and across the library, moving as quietly as she could so as not to disturb her host.

She paused midway through though, and turned around. She re-examined the chess board carved into the floor. One of the tiles, the White Queen, had been *moved*. She looked again and again, even circling the "board" a few times. It was impossible, of course. The tiles were quite literally the floor of the room. And yet, every part of her screamed that the tile had been in a different square earlier in the day. Helen took a long slow breath, closed her eyes, and let it slowly out before turning toward the kitchen and stepping off. She was wrong, that's all. She had to be. There wasn't any other explanation, really.

The lighting in the house was still fairly even, and Helen was surprised that they left so many lamps on throughout the night. Then again, perhaps they'd done so for her benefit.

By the time she reached the dining room, she'd put the bizarre happening on the stairwell to the back of her mind, and was entirely focused on the divine smell emanating from beyond the heavy door. A place setting remained at the ready for her, though this time it was a simpler setup. She smiled at Luciana's thoughtfulness, and made her way to the kitchen door at the back of the room.

She pulled it open without a thought, and it swung silently on well oiled hinges. A distant orange light caught her eye at once, a row of glowing symbols hovering in the air over the counter across the room.

She squinted in disbelief as rows of unfamiliar reddish orange symbols swirled through the air above an ancient cast iron stove.

Helen screwed her eyes shut and shook her head, even going so far as to rub her eyes vigorously, and sure enough when she opened them the glowing orange letters were revealed to be the clock face above a perfectly normal, brushed metal range.

"Fuck," she rubbed her temples. "Keep it together, Helen. What the hell am I going to do without my meds."

Tick-tock, tick-tock.

Shut up.

Helen stepped up to the oven, which had a pair of floral, green-and-white oven mitts atop it, and pulled the door open.

A covered red ceramic dish greeted her. Upon inspection it contained the promised risotto, a creamy, parsley-topped masterpiece that smelled of garlic and onion.

In fact, from what she could see, the dish hadn't been touched. Which, she realized guiltily, meant that it had been made specifically for her consumption. She cradled it in two hands and carefully brought it out to the table where she set it down on the trivet already laid out. There was a serving spoon as well, so she dished herself a small serving.

It was thick, aromatic, and as the note had warned, it was piping hot. She opted to let her food cool, and returned to the kitchen to scrounge up something to drink. A bottle of chilled Riesling in the fridge found its way into her hands, but she couldn't find the wine glasses, so she decided a coffee mug would have to do.

She was headed back to the dining room when she noticed a bowl of uncooked rice on the granite counter beside a wide-bodied metal sink.

She strode over and examined it more closely. Setting her drink down, she dug a hand into the rice and sure enough, she pulled out her phone a moment later. It was scratched to hell and the screen was cracked in one corner, but otherwise it seemed fine. She pressed the power button, but it was either broken or out of battery, because it didn't so much as blip with life.

"Damn," she sighed, laying it back down and returning to her wine. "Old school land line it is, for now."

She pushed back through the door to the dining room a moment later, and nearly jumped out of her skin to find Luciana sitting at the table in a black silk nightgown. The lace trimmed garment clung scandalously to her lithe physique, and it ended just past the middle of her thighs.

"Hello, Helen," she grinned broadly. "Did you sleep well?"

"I- yes, I did," Helen managed, her temperature rising. "A little too well, I think. I seem to have missed dinner."

"You had a trying day yesterday, your body must've needed the rest, that's all."

Helen swallowed the lump in her throat and struggled to tear her gaze away from the inky, star speckled darkness of Luciana's eyes.

"Please, don't let me stop you," her host patted the table. "You should eat."

Helen sat compulsively, there was a power in Luciana's voice that couldn't be denied. Goosebumps broke out all along her arms and legs as her hostess scooted closer in the semi-darkness.

"I am sorry for not waking you," Luciana shrugged apologetically. "You looked quite peaceful."

"My dad always used to say 'you must've needed the rest champ' any time I overslept."

"Used to?"

"He… passed away when I was younger."

"I'm sorry to hear that," Luciana looked down, tracing her fingers across the grain of the wooden table. "Losing a parent is… hard."

"It's been a long time," Helen said with a reassuring smile. "I've more or less come to terms, I think."

"Even so, we never really heal from a wound like that, do we?"

Helen felt herself choking up in a way she hadn't in years. She was surprised at herself as tears began to swell behind her eyes.

"Yes, I'm.. I suppose you're right," she cleared her throat and shook her head. "Th-thank you for letting me sleep. And for leaving dinner for me. And, well for everything."

"It's such an incredibly rare treat to have a guest, it's my pleasure."

"I'm honestly surprised you're awake," Helen furrowed her brow as a thought occurred. "I didn't wake you, did I?"

Luciana's burst of tickled laughter was like the sparkle of Christmas lights - dazzling, enchanting, and full of honest joy.

"W-what did I say?" Helen couldn't help but smile back.

"You're just such a thoughtful person."

Luciana reached over and tucked a strand of stray hair behind Helen's ear, and in so doing stole her breath away. Her fingers were warm and silky soft as they lightly grazed Helen's cheek. She smelled of warm vanilla and cinnamon, a heady, intoxicating scent that gripped her heart and clouded her mind.

The moment lingered like the warmth of Luciana's touch, but eventually the captivating woman leaned back into her chair and broke the silence.

"I get quite... energetic at night," she smiled wickedly. "Something about the stars and the moonlight stirs my blood."

The soft roll of her accent and the light in her eyes was offset - only slightly - by the faintest hint of... Helen struggled to place the feeling. She felt like a deer staring into the eyes of a mountain lion, unsure whether it was hungry.

"I, uh," Helen gulped subconsciously. "I have trouble sleeping, too."

"Oh I don't mind sleeping," Luciana stood up and paced restlessly. "But some nights there's just so much *power* in the air, you know?"

She turned back to Helen with a fierce shine in her eyes.

"I do," Helen all but whispered, the words resonating within her insomnia-ridden mind.

"Ah, forgive my rudeness," Luciana put a palm to her forehead. "Eat, *eat*, you must be starving. I'll leave you alone and we can-"

"No," Helen stuck out her hand, urging her host to stay. "Um, you could, ah, sit with me? Tell me more about yourself, and this place."

"Are you sure?"

"Positive."

Luciana insisted on serving up a more generous portion of the slowly cooling risotto for her guest before she sat herself and adjusted the hem of her nightgown, which Helen noticed had ridden several inches up her thighs.

"Not a word until you take a bite," Luciana ordered, her quirked eyebrow and crooked smile juxtaposing the power that once again underlined her words.

Helen caved immediately.

She brought the polished silver spoon to her lips and took a bite. She was overwhelmed immediately by the complex flavors and smooth texture of the dish, and couldn't help but close her eyes in delight as she savored it.

"Good?"

"Unbelievable," Helen nodded. "Honestly."

"Great," Luciana let loose her sparkling smile once more. "So, I guess I could start with how I came to be here, yes?"

Helen nodded, but kept eating.

"Well, I can say I never expected to be in Oklahoma, " she smiled wistfully. "I wanted to live further south, where I spent most of my life."

Helen noticed a certain melancholy growing in her eyes.

"But there were some... family issues," her smile grew bitter. "And so I made the decision to leave. To leave and never look back."

"I-I'm sorry," Helen looked down at the table.

"Not your fault," Luciana's smile was less warm now. "It was something I'd foreseen. Something I watched develop for many years and chose to ignore in the hopes that I was wrong."

Helen took another bite to fill the silence, but Luciana was lost in thought.

"So you're from Texas then?"

"Hmm?"

"You said you were from further south. It doesn't get much further south than Oklahoma."

"Well, I never actually said I was American."

Helen's cheeks glowed.

"Oh my God," she groaned, putting a palm to her forehead. "That's embarrassing."

Luciana laughed, leaned slightly forward, and gave Helen a playful nudge.

Helen smiled, but the simple gesture had left her breathless. Had it been her imagination, or did the other woman's fingers linger a moment on the soft skin of her shoulder?

"No need for embarrassment, it's a common assumption. Or it was back when I went out more."

"So, where are you from?"

"Oh," a tinge of pink rose in Luciana's cheeks. "Er, Europe, actually, but I left a very, very long time ago. "

"Do you miss it?"

"In some ways, yes, but I've found a great deal of peace here over the years as well. Now I can't imagine ever leaving this place."

"I wish I had a place that felt that safe," Helen mumbled.

"Someday," Luciana smiled. "I hope you will."

"Maybe," Helen thought of her mother's house and frowned. "It just feels like such an... I don't know, unrealistic dream, I guess."

"There's magic in our thoughts, Helen," Luciana locked eyes with her and Helen was surprised by her sudden intensity. "Our thoughts have the power to shape our destinies."

Helen searched Luciana's face and found only fierce conviction. The pair held each other's gaze for a long moment before Luciana broke away.

"I'm sorry," she stood. "I'm interrupting your meal, babbling on like this."

"Please stay," Helen said, this time with more confidence. "I'd love to hear more about you, and about this place."

Clingy. Pathetic.

"Well," Luciana blushed delicately in the dim lighting. "I'm really not *that* interesting, but I'm happy to answer your questions."

A million questions flooded Helen's mind, and one by one they were rejected as she struggled with her self doubt. As the silence between them lengthened, she became increasingly aware of the awkwardness of the silence until she at last blurted out the next thing on her mind.

"The chess set!"

"Sorry?"

"The, uh," Helen pointed at the door. "The chess set on the floor of the library. It, uh, well I mean I *thought* it looked different this morning?"

"Different how," Luciana answered slowly, her eyes narrowing ever-so-slightly.

"The white queen was in f5," she replied softly. "It was threatening both of black's bishops in f3 and c5, but now it's *in* c5 and black's queen-side is just gone."

Luciana looked conflicted, but for the life of her, Helen couldn't figure out why.

"I take it you're a chess player then?"

Helen nodded, trying not to feel too frustrated at the way Luciana apparently dismissed her question.

"I'm something of a casual fan myself," the woman looked away. "Not even close to the best player I know, of course."

"So the board in the library *isn't* just for show," Helen pressed. "It's actually a functional board?"

"It is," her host's smile seemed a bit forced now. "It was built by… the original architect. I use it every once in a while, I'm sorry if it took you off guard."

"It's flawless, I never would've known if the pieces hadn't moved."

"You are extremely perceptive, and I am sorry I didn't think to mention it before to save you the confusion."

"Who are you playing against, if I might ask?"

"You'll think it's silly."

"No, I promise it isn't as-"

"Myself," she grinned sheepishly. "I'm actually playing a match against myself right now."

"You know, that's far more common than you might think," Helen beamed. "I'm just glad I'm not losing my mind."

"I get nervous around anyone who hasn't lost at least a little of their mind," Luciana laughed, her humor returning and her attitude once again warm and inviting. "They're not to be trusted, don't you think?"

"I dunno," Helen's smile faltered. "Being crazy isn't all it's cracked up to be."

"Oh?"

Helen gave a wry half-smile and shrugged her shoulders in response.

"Should I be concerned?" Luciana winked playfully. "You're not an ax murderer, are you?"

Yet.

Shut up.

"No, no, nothing like that. I just... I'm," Helen's carefully built defenses struggled mightily against her desire to trust the beautiful, kind woman in front of her.

"Helen," Luciana scooted closer and put a hand on her shoulder. "You don't owe me an explanation."

"I d-do, though," Helen sighed and hung her head. "My medication was in that car, and without it I'm less... stable?"

"We'll get you through-"

"It isn't the kind of thing you can 'push through,'" Helen air-quoted. "More like the 'when people find out they get nervous' kind of thing."

She'll abandon you, why wouldn't she?

"So you're afraid you're a...," Luciana paused, her eyes unreadable. "In danger or perhaps *a* danger?"

"I-well."

"Because if you're worried about *me*, I want to reassure you that-"

Don't do it-

"I'm bipolar," Helen blurted in a rush, compelled by her anxieties to alert this woman to the burden she represented. "And um, my condition isn't well… uh *well-controlled*."

Silence.

Here it comes.

"That's a… challenging condition, and I am sorry you have to deal with that, but in *this* house, you are not alone. You don't have to do this by yourself."

Helen smiled as tears threatened to break out from her watery eyes.

"I-"

"Helen," Luciana reached a hand out to lift Helen's chin, bringing them face to face and eye to eye. "Is there a reason you feel you have to tell me this?"

"I just," Helen looked at the ground as the weight of her self-loathing dragged her gaze downward. "I thought you should know if I'm going to be staying here."

"I admit I don't know much about bipolar disorder," Luciana's speckled gold and brown eyes were endless and mesmerizing. "But I'm a quick study and more importantly I'm not going anywhere, ok?"

Helen nodded.

"Good," she let go of Helen's chin and sat up straighter. "What do I *need* to know, that you're comfortable sharing?"

Helen straightened up as well. The absence of Luciana's warm hand and strong fingers left her feeling a peculiar emptiness and with a growing warmth in her chest.

"Well, it's a bit... unpredictable," Helen rubbed her temples. "My medications were in my car and without them it's kind of a roll of the dice whether I go up, down, or stay level."

Luciana's eyes were locked on to Helen's, and they were filled with kindness, and without a shadow of judgment.

"I...s-sometimes have a little trouble distinguishing what's real from what isn't," she blushed. "It's not like I see dragons flying around or the sky turns purple, it's more like... well, sometimes things look like they shouldn't, or do things they aren't supposed to. It's hard to explain."

She paused for a moment, casting about for a concrete example.

"Like earlier, I swear your chess board sculpture thing moved," she laughed nervously, trying to ignore the brief moment when Luciana's eyes widened.

"Well, any time you have a doubt about what's real," Luciana winked. "You can trust me to give it to you straight. Anything else?"

"No, I don't think so," Helen smiled half-heartedly.

"Helen, I don't want you to worry," Luciana's tone was serious now. "You're safe here with me."

"I really am grateful, Luciana," Helen's shoulders dropped with relief. "And I know you said there is no debt or whatever but-"

Luciana raised a finger and shook her head.

"Right," Helen sighed. "There is no debt."

"That's right," Luciana smiled. "Now, I really ought to leave you be if you're to eat and get some rest."

"I really don't mind," Helen protested weakly. "I think you're fascinating."

She blushed, regretting her word choice despite Luciana's kind, honest laughter.

"As are you."

Luciana leaned over and kissed Helen softly on the forehead, her warm lips starting a chain reaction that set Helen's whole body tingling.

"Good night."

Helen was speechless, she simply watched dumbfounded as she stepped nimbly from the room, closing the door behind herself.

Helen was frozen for what felt like several minutes. All the gears in her mind had ground to a screeching halt the moment Luciana's lips had touched her skin.

She was pulled back to reality by a loud gurgle from her stomach, but even as she tucked into her risotto, she couldn't take her mind off her host. The more she dwelt on the warmth of those lips, the bounce of her ebony curls, the smell of cinnamon that surrounded her, and the mesmerizing way she moved, the less clearly she could think.

She ate a little more, and finished a second mug of wine, but she found that her hunger for food was largely gone - replaced by a craving she knew she couldn't indulge. Eventually, she pushed back from the table, collected her dishes, and headed back to the kitchen. Helen pushed the door open and jumped in surprise at the sight of Armand, who was waiting patiently by the sink. The man still wore his suit, but had a neat white apron on over it.

"I can take those for you, ma'am," he said in the same soft and even tone. "I would be happy to wash them for you."

"S-sure," she stammered, handing the dishes over before taking a step back.

"Would the lady prefer to finish her wine?"

Helen looked back and forth from Armand to the bottle of wine and wine glass that he held in one hand.

"Actually, er, yes please."

She took the wine and bottle and waited, but the man simply stood staring at her until she gave an awkward sort of nod and spun on her heel to leave. She resisted the urge to look back until she'd made it to the library, and when she did the hallway was empty.

Unthinking, Helen walked directly through the center of the room and was startled when her foot caught on something on the floor. She looked down and realized she was in the middle of the chess set.

"How *do* you work?" she muttered, pushing up her glasses before bending down to inspect the icons on the floor.

Each "piece" was an individual metal disk emblazoned with a raised symbol. She'd stepped on the white queen in c5, which had definitely moved since earlier. She reached out, expecting the piece to lift from the floor, but it didn't budge. She tugged harder, then pulled with all her strength but the thing wouldn't move.

Helen set down her wine and glass and looked around for a mechanism that might operate the board, but nothing stood out.

"What the hell," she frowned, before lighting up with an idea. "Queen to c6!"

Nothing.

"Well, that was stupid," she glanced around to make sure no one had seen her.

Helen scooped up her beverage, poured half a glass, and then headed to the stairs as she took a sip. By the time she made it to the second floor her glass was in need of a refill, so she obliged on the way to her room.

She was surprised at how tired she still was, especially considering her extended nap earlier, but the more she drank the heavier her eyelids grew. She set the glass and bottle down on the nightstand and pulled herself into bed, snuggling down into the heavy comforter and closing her eyes.

It wasn't wine, chess, or even the disconcerting face of Armand that filled her mind as she drifted off - it was bouncing black curls, soft caramel skin, and piercing eyes flecked with gold.

Chapter Four

Helen woke, half expecting the events of the past day and a half to have been a dream. But no, she was in the same messy bed she'd fallen asleep in, deep within Casa De Rosas. Sunlight pierced through the gloom of the past two days, sending sunbeams dancing across the bed and along the perfectly set floorboards, bringing a sense of relief to Helen's stormy mind. Moments later a particularly strong gust of wind sent a sheet of rain hammering against the side of the house though, reminding her that they had not yet seen the last of the ugly weather.

She climbed out of bed and headed for one of the windows. She tugged the lace curtains aside and peered out. The sun was not visible, but bits of its radiance competed with the gloomy gray cloud cover to speckle the grounds below. The rain was not nearly the intensity it had been the previous two days, but it was still something between a shower and a downpour.

A few holes appeared in the cloud cover above as she watched, sending glowing beams of sunlight down to earth. She gasped at the beauty of one of her favorite natural phenomena and stayed glued to the window until the clouds shifted again, closing the holes and cloaking the ground in gloom once more.

Helen sighed wistfully and headed for the door. She pulled it open and promptly jumped back in surprise.

"Good morning, madam," Armand bowed stiffly. "The Lady suggested that you might wish to wear something else. I am to direct you to her wardrobe, if you wish."

"Jesus, how long have you-"

She paused, replaying what he'd said several times in her head.

"You mean... you mean *her* closet with *her* clothes?"

"Yes ma'am."

"I, uh... sure?"

Armand turned without another word and headed down the hallway at a modest pace.

Where does she sleep anyway?

They reached the landing, but rather than turn toward the stairway, the pale, slender man turned to the nondescript wooden double doors. He approached them, and pulled on the peculiar metal rings that served as door handles. They swung wide to reveal a small antechamber that had an archway at the other end, opening up into a larger room.

Helen paused, expecting her guide to enter first, but he stayed where he was, staring at her calmly.

"D-do you go first or?"

"I am not permitted in the Lady's chambers," he said flatly. "I have not been invited."

"So…," she looked at him meaningfully, but he remained silent. "Ok then."

Helen stepped across the threshold and onto the dark-stained wood of the antechamber. She turned at the sound of a soft click and was unnerved to find that Armand had shut the doors behind her.

"It's not weird," she muttered, taking a timid step forward. "Definitely not weird."

A few more steps took her to the main room, or rather one of them. It looked as though there were at least two more doors leading elsewhere. It was *impossible*, however, to contemplate where they might lead in light of the... distractions that abounded in the bedroom.

The floors were more of the immaculate hardwood, and the dark walls matched the rest of the house, but the accents were... bold.

One wall held a pair of large ebony dressers with gold hardware - real gold from the looks of it - and each held an assortment of candles and small boxes. The wall above the dresser held not only more art, but also Helen's rapt attention. Three long rectangular paintings hung side by side, all depicting the same two young women. Moreover, they depicted in exquisite detail the various stages and forms of ecstasy shared between them. The curve of arched backs, the fine red scratch lines on a lover's skin, the curled toes and half-closed eyes, all paired with the most delicate wrinkles of sheets and impossibly perfect lighting. Helen's neck warmed, and she found herself breathing heavier as a familiar desire grew within herself.

Two *women*, she chewed her lip as she drew closer for a better look. Could her host's taste in the sapphic mean that - no, she refused even to consider it. She dragged her mind back to the present and spun around for something else to look at.

Her eyes fell on the massive bed - its frame was of heavy black metal, while the sheets and pillows were a dark, blood red satin. The massive four-poster was adorned with shiny black satin curtains, and each of the four columns that held the canopy aloft was a life-size sculpture of a nude woman with her arms stretched above her head.

Helen's mind be damned, her feet pulled her closer to the bed until she was just beside it. Without taking her eyes from the sculptures she reached out and felt the bedspread and was unsurprised to find it was fine silk.

At this distance, the columns looked for all the world like dark black metal maidens frozen in time. She reached to touch one but her foot caught on something, pulling her gaze downward. The space under the bed was odd, it almost looked like a large cage or kennel - but Helen hadn't seen any sign of dogs in the manor so far.

A soft click behind her caused Helen to jump. She took a guilty step backwards from the bed and spun around. Her face was flushed from more than embarrassment, so she was relieved to not see anyone. Looking this way and that, she was unable to see what might've made the click until - had that door been ajar before?

A wooden door off to one side of the bed, initially unnoticed, was cracked open an inch or so.

"Hmm," she looked around again to ensure she was alone and then moved across the room. "I suppose I'll have to open doors to find a closet, right?"

The door swung open easily at her gentle tug, and a light flickered on automatically to reveal a large walk-in closet.

"Bingo."

The room was perhaps fifteen feet by fifteen feet, and while the upper half was all hanging garments and accessories, the bottom half was drawers and dressers of various sizes and shapes. Helen reached up to the first top she found and tugged it into the light, it was a formal white blouse that didn't seem to match her host's fashion at all.

She worked her way around the room, looking through clothes both formal and casual - though all definitively stylish - until she was about halfway through the collection. Here there was a section of purses, clutches, belts and the like. She skimmed past those and then stopped dead in her tracks.

She was staring directly at a black lace bodysuit. The garment was designed to conceal only the most *specific* of areas, with the winding, curling lace accenting the curves and lines of the body. That must mean that the next section, if the first item were any indicator, was lingerie.

A clear and intimate image of her host wearing the bodysuit immediately invaded her mind and Helen's knees went weak for a second.

She savored the image for a moment, then quickly scanned the section. It was… sizable. Helen felt heat moving through her body as she stole a glance behind herself and then pressed onward into the collection.

By the time she got to the first dresser in the section, she was practically vibrating with desire. She pulled open the top drawer of one of the dressers expecting to find… well honestly anything. Even with her open mind, she was taken aback. On one side there were a variety of exquisite heels, and on the other there were sleek coils of silk rope.

"Having trouble finding something you like?"

Helen whipped around, slamming the drawer shut as she did so, and felt her face go scarlet. Luciana, standing in the doorway wearing a tightly clinging off-white sundress, had an irresistible curl in her smile.

"W-well, I was uhm, I ah-"

"Browsing?"

The woman's voice was buttery soft, but it held Helen's mind in an iron grip.

Helen's breath caught as she stared unabashedly, drinking in the long toned legs, the flaring hips, the smoothly muscled arms and the well-defined bust of her host.

She couldn't bring herself to speak, the lump in her throat was too hard to swallow, but she dumbly nodded.

"I was thinking of changing as well, actually," Luciana took a heart-stopping step closer. "You don't mind, do you?"

"M-mind? Do I mind what?"

Her laugh was intoxicating.

"If I change."

"Here," Helen managed faintly. "Now?"

"I'm not shy," Luciana drew closer, until less than a foot separated them. "Are you?"

Helen was lost so deep in the gold-flecked depths of her eyes, she couldn't even begin to answer, not until Luciana reached up and ran a long slim finger up her jaw bone, then across her cheek to tuck another strand of hair behind her ear.

Her touch shot lightning bolts through Helen's body, stoking the fire inside her to an inferno that had her clenching her hands into fists and digging her nails into her palms.

"Yes, I mean no, I mean I d-don't mind," Helen stammered, fighting the urge to kiss those full, pouty lips.

"Perhaps you can give me a hand then," Luciana smiled, dazzling her once again.

The woman turned around, showing Helen her back, and reached up to lift her curly hair to reveal a simple bow holding up her sundress.

"Could you untie me?"

Helen gulped and raised her trembling hands. Luciana was a fair bit taller than she was, but it was a simple matter to pull the twin cotton strings apart. The knot slipped loose with ease and Luciana's dress dropped several inches. Her bare back was smooth and relatively unblemished, with the exception of three, inch-wide scars, evenly spaced perhaps two inches apart, that ran diagonally from her right shoulder toward her left hip.

Helen's fingers lingered after completing their task, and she ran them lightly down Luciana's shoulders to trace the scars but Luciana spun around. Her eyes were, for a moment, stained with sadness. Helen was too captivated by the fact that the only thing holding up her host's sundress was one arm across her breasts.

"You're-"

Helen's observation was interrupted as Luciana moved her hand and her sundress dropped to the floor in one fluid movement.

"Beautiful," she breathed. "You're beautiful."

Luciana's body brought to mind an amazon - the perfect combination of form and function, beauty and strength, grace and desire. Her stomach was toned, but healthy, and marred only by a roughly tennis-ball sized scar on her right side.

Helen's gaze didn't linger though as she was drawn to those hips that dipped just *so*. Her breasts, full and ripe as honeydews, moved gently with each of her deep, even breaths, and a short cropped tuft of jet black hair graced the space between her thighs. Everything from her shoulders to her calves radiated a certain... power, the strength of an athlete hidden beneath the kind exterior of a gentle woman.

"And yet I find myself at a disadvantage," Luciána purred. "I'm in a rather... vulnerable position compared to you, at the moment."

Helen, still wearing the same flannel pajamas, couldn't grip the hem of her shirt fast enough. She reached down and yanked the garment up over her head. In her haste, she caught her glasses and pulled herself off-balance.

Strong, warm arms gripped her around the waist before she could fall and she froze. She was exposed from the waist up except her eyes, which were still covered by the shirt, and her arms which were tangled overhead.

"Careful now," Luciana murmured directly into her ear. "There's no need to rush."

She felt herself being gently pushed and responded by stepping back until she found herself up against the wall between racks of clothing. The cool plaster stood in stark contrast to Luciana, whose body now gently pressed against her own. Breast against breast, stomach to stomach, she could feel Luciana's breath almost as easily as she could feel her own pounding heart.

Luciana's hands gripped her hips with unexpected strength, pushing her more firmly against the wall and turning her inside molten.

Helen gasped unconsciously, and she swore she could *feel* Luciana smile in return.

"Allow me."

Luciana's hands ran slowly, inexorably up her sides. Every inch drove Helen mad as she teased her way up to Helen's breasts. She half expected Luciana to touch her there, to take her smaller, perkier breasts in hand - but she didn't. She slipped past as though the thought had never occurred to her.

Helen let out a whimper of disappointment, but if Luciana reacted it wasn't verbally.

Luciana's journey of exploration continued until at long last, after tracing Helen's shoulders and running her fingers along her slender throat she reached the flannel shirt.

Continuing her trend of driving Helen mad, she lifted the shirt slowly - and carefully - past Helen's glasses and then up over her arms. With nowhere else to go, Helen let her arms fall across Luciana's shoulders in a not-so-subtle effort to continue their embrace.

"I think I'd like to kiss you," she blurted out, biting her lip.

Luciana leaned in, her lips gently parted, but instead of meeting Helen's hungry mouth, she drew close to her left ear.

"Then do it."

In a single heartbeat, Helen pulled them together with force, closing the short gap between their waiting lips. Their lips met, their tongues dancing with a wild, youthful vigor for what felt like an eternity before Helen was forced to come up for air. She threw her head back and shuddered as Luciana's hungry lips moved to her neck.

Luciana's hands slid down Helen's back until they reached her flannel-clad rear. Her firm squeeze elicited a giggle from Helen that quickly turned to a gasp of surprise as Luciana lifted the smaller woman up in one fluid motion.

Perhaps it was the effortless strength, or perhaps it was simply her desire, but Helen instinctively wrapped her legs around her host. Her core was on fire and she found herself pressing and squeezing so as to slowly grind her center against her host's firm abdomen.

"Should we move somewhere more comfortable?" her host breathed in a voice heavy with desire.

"Mmm, I've got a place in mind," Helen responded timidly, glancing out the closet door at the bed waiting some twenty feet away. "If, if you want."

"I can honestly tell you I want *nothing* more."

Luciana met her gaze and Helen was amazed to see that some trick of the light had given her eyes the faintest pink and purple flecks where the gold had been only minutes before.

"Sh-should I walk?"

"You don't like being carried?" Luciana looked a little surprised.

"Oh n-no," Helen gave her a quick reassuring kiss. "I'm loving it actually I just didn't know if I was too… heavy?"

Luciana's laugh once again drove her mad. It was so rich and kind and carefree.

"Not a chance."

True to her word, Luciana barely seemed to notice Helen's weight as she delicately moved through the doorway to the side of the bed. If she was straining at all, Helen couldn't tell. Then again, she found herself distracted by every inch of the woman carrying her - not to mention the unfamiliar feeling of being *cradled.*

Luciana's long legs carried them swiftly to the bed where Helen found herself gracefully set down upon the edge with her feet dangling above the floor. From her seated perspective, Luciana towered over her and to her surprise Helen enjoyed the feeling of powerlessness that washed over her.

"What now?"

"That depends on you," Luciana leaned forward, her eyes hungry and bright. "We could simply change our clothes and go, perhaps enjoy a quiet breakfast together or…"

"Or," Helen responded, a little too eagerly to be ignored. "Or what?"

Luciana placed a hand on either side of Helen's hips and leaned in even closer.

"Or I could bring you pleasure 'til you scream," she whispered. "We can share each other's bodies until we're both sore and our muscles are too tired to move, and *then* we can think about food."

Speechless, Helen simply nodded.

Luciana pressed forward, giving Helen an unexpectedly tender kiss. The kiss grew more fervent and passionate but just as Helen was really leaning into it, she felt a strong hand on the middle of her chest.

Helen allowed herself to be pushed backwards until she was laying on the bed, her hips at the edge and her legs hanging over the side.

Their kiss now broken, Luciana's lips danced across Helen's neck and collar bones. Everywhere she went she left heat and warmth, followed by the cold of the cool air touching the moisture her attention left behind.

Around and around she went, moving under, over, and beside Helen's breasts but never gracing them directly with her attention. Already Helen's body ached, her back arching and her hands gripping the bedspread like a vice.

"Please," she moaned, surprising even herself.

She could feel Luciana smile even as she moved at last to Helen's pert nipples. Her soft tongue rolled across Helen's areola in lazy circles, brushing gently against her nipple and sending shots of lightning across Helen's chest and down between her thighs where she was already soaking wet.

Another few delicious moments were spent between her nipples before Luciana moved at last down Helen's stomach. She paused to savor the dips that led down her hips and between her thighs - at least as far as she could access while Helen was still clothed.

"May I?"

"Mhmm," was all the response she could manage.

Luciana's fingers moved gently but with purpose as they gripped the hem of her pants on either side. She pulled them down in tantalizing, slow fashion to reveal Helen's own clean-shaven mound.

Helen could feel the cool air against her thighs. It contrasted with the warmth of Luciana's hands upon her knees and the heat of her breath, which matched the warmth of her core, now within easy reach of her companion's talented mouth.

Luciana paused between her legs and Helen opened her half-closed eyes, both hands gripping the silky soft sheets with a death grip in anticipation. She found herself acutely lucid. Everything stood in sharp contrast, as though someone had turned up the brightness on the world. The cloth beneath her naked back, the pain of biting her lip to keep from crying out, and the dazzling white pattern of symbols inscribed around the edges of the canopy above her. The most acute sensations, however, were the strong warmth of those hands, and the-

Helen gasped as Luciana pulled her knees apart with sudden force, exposing her fully. She barely had time to catch her breath when she felt that warm probing tongue and those sumptuous lips working their way up her inner thigh.

Helen's will to be silent was broken as Luciana enveloped her vulva without warning. She bit her lip hard enough to bleed and then cried out

as the talented woman between her thighs dragged her strong tongue up and down her slit. She alternated swirling gently in figure eights around her clit and penetrating her depths.

Luciana enjoyed her with reckless abandon and Helen's inner thighs were swiftly dripping wet. She felt her climax building like a tidal wave but her brain couldn't process fast enough to communicate it to her partner. Instead, her eyes rolled back in her head as she began to shudder all over.

When the wave finally crashed, she cried out once more, squeezing her thighs together and reaching down with one hand to grip the back of Luciana's head. Rather than pull back, her partner pressed harder, riding wave after wave as she bucked and rolled.

"T-too, too m-much," she managed at last between ragged breaths.

Luciana drew back, her cheeks and chin and lips soaked with her lover and a broad smile on her face.

"Oh my god," Helen breathed heavily. "I don't think I've *ever* felt like that befo-"

Helen felt herself suddenly lifted and pushed back on the bed as Luciana climbed up to position herself over her.

"My turn?" she asked, an eyebrow raised quizzically. "Or are you spent?"

"My pleasure," Helen blushed heavily. "But I'm n-not sure I can measure up to what you just did."

"We've all the time in the world to practice," Luciana purred, reaching down and picking up one of Helen's hands.

Helen allowed her hand to be guided first to Luciana's breast, which was full and soft and warm like the most perfect pillow, then down her firm muscled stomach, and finally down between her legs.

"I-"

"Just explore," Luciana smiled, putting her at ease. "If you're nervous."

Helen closed her eyes and allowed herself to focus on her other senses. She could feel the short-cropped, surprisingly soft hair, the gentle slope of Luciana's vulva.

Oh, *that* got a reaction.

She rubbed her hand across the center of her lover, her index and middle fingers discovering a slit of warmth and wetness that they paused to contemplate. She dug deeper, running her fingers between slick lips and probing a moment more to locate Luciana's clit. She circled it with soft gentle finger strokes and she could feel the woman above her shudder with pleasure.

Unwilling to cut straight to the chase without providing some measure of the enjoyment that she'd received, she moved further down and slipped two fingers into her lover, eliciting a gasp that turned into a moan as she curled the digits in a come-hither motion, probing her tight, wet walls while seeking out the firmer, rougher patch of her partner's g-spot.

With every stroke Luciana pushed back harder and harder, rocking her body to meet Helen's fingers. Her breath grew ragged and short as Helen incorporated her thumb to press and pamper Luciana's clit. The rocking motion of her lover above was counterbalanced by Helen's hand, ensuring that the maximum pressure was felt both internally and externally with every wave.

Helen opened her eyes to see Luciana, eyes closed, panting above her with her arms trembling and sweat upon her brow. Helen craned her neck up the few inches it took to meet her lover's face and engaged her in another passionate kiss, her hand never ceasing its work. Her plan worked, and as she laid her head back down Luciana followed. Their tongues danced and Helen could taste herself even as Luciana's movements became more erratic and convulsive. Finally, in a climax of sound and movement, she cried out and pressed hard against Helen's hand. She ground against her for several more shuddering moments until she lay still at last.

Moments passed as she recovered before she pushed herself back to all fours and met Helen's gaze.

Helen bit her lip in exaggerated nervousness and stared back at her unblinking host.

"Was that… alright?"

"Yes, yes," Luciana chuckled past heavy breaths. "Yeah, that was definitely 'alright.'"

"Should we… go get that breakfast now or?"

"Oh my sweet lover. We're just getting started, aren't we?"

Chapter Five

"You worked up quite an appetite," Luciana teased as Helen popped another strawberry into her mouth.

Helen grinned sheepishly, but snagged another of the berries off the platter between them. The pair were tucked away, just off the main bedroom, in a cozy nook that held a few potted plants, a small table, two chairs, and a bay window that doubtless would've had a stunning view if not for the rain.

Helen blushed and smiled, a trickle of juice running out of the side of her mouth. She reached to brush it away but Luciana beat her to it, running a finger up her chin to collect the bright red liquid before bringing it to her mouth.

"I'm surprised you're not eating *more*," Helen countered to cover the red in her cheeks. "You did most of the heavy lifting."

"You're hardly what I would call heavy lifting."

Damn that sparkling laugh, Helen was sure it would echo in her mind forever.

"In fact, you're fairly light."

"What, is there like a gym around here or something?"

Luciana paused and looked awkwardly at a loss for words.

"Err, yes, well yes of course there's a gym... downstairs."

"Downstairs? Doesn't the staircase stop at the library? What's lower than that?"

"Ah, no," Luciana resumed her normal confidence. "No, it goes down to a lower level with a gym and a wine cellar."

"Huh. I can't believe I-"

"Let's take a walk," Luciana stood suddenly, the thin silk robe she wore flashing in the intermittent rays of morning light pouring in through the windows.

The woman held her hand out and Helen took it with a smile.

Both of them were in brightly colored, mid-thigh length kimonos with gold accents - Luciana in red while Helen wore deep royal purple. Helen allowed herself to be led through the rest of the bedroom suite, then down the stairs to the library and towards the main doors. She took the opportunity to glance over at the stairs and was puzzled to see that the stairs in fact did continue further down, despite her memories to the contrary.

Luciana's firm hand tugged her away from the staircase, however, and they made their way barefoot down a marble-tiled hall to the stately main entrance to the manor. Even having seen it the day before on her tour, Helen marveled at the dark red wood, delicately carved to resemble trees flanking a large double-door of the same wide-grained wood.

Helen reached for the heavy golden handle only to pull her hand back in surprise as it was opened from the outside.

"Madam, Miss Helen," Armand, immaculate as ever, bowed low as he held open the portal. "Please, allow me."

"How does he *do* that?" Helen whispered as the two stepped out onto the rough-cut stone outside the door.

"He's built for the job," her host whispered back conspiratorially before slipping past Helen with a giggle.

Helen allowed herself to be dragged into the shallow shelter of a large red-tiled awning that stretched out beyond the entrance in a wide semi-circle. Beyond their small haven, the rain was still steadily beating down on the grounds, even as the skies above taunted onlookers with glimpses of bright, sunny blue.

"Now what?"

Luciana didn't answer except by taking a deep, slow breath.

"Luciana?"

"Breathe. Feel the power in the thunder," her words were punctuated with eerie accuracy by a crackle of distant thunder. "And the life in the rains."

Helen closed her eyes, acutely aware of the soft hand that held her own, and tried her best to focus. A dozen sounds, from birdsong to the staccato of the rain on the tile roof, all vied for her attention and try as she might she couldn't force herself to-

"Relax, Helen," Helen felt Luciana's warm hand on her cheek. "*Breathe*."

Helen let out the breath she hadn't realized she was holding and, rather than focus on removing everything else, she simply focused on her breaths. Nothing changed, at first. As time moved at an immeasurably pace, she slowly began to feel a tug, a gentle ebb and flow, all around her body and beyond. The air itself danced with a purpose across her, caressing her exposed thighs and toying with her messy hair.

"Do you feel it?"

"I-I think so?"

Helen furrowed her brow as the feelings intensified. She felt herself compelled to turn as a momentum built inside her and she finally snapped

112

open her eyes with a gasp. Directly in front of her a massive arcing fork of lightning struck a hillside not far away and the accompanying thunder shook the ground, drawing with it much of the energy that she had felt building.

This isn't right, this isn't real, Helen.

"Helen? What's wrong-"

Helen turned on her heel, her heart racing, and yanked open the door to the mansion before bolting inside. She broke into a run, ignoring the confused cries of her host as she turned the corner into the library. She would've kept going but, in her haste, she once again forgot the chessboard that decorated the space.

Helen caught her big toe on the edge of a piece and tumbled across the tiles in an ignoble heap, glasses skittering away. She slid to the edge of the room and bumped into a bookcase where she pulled her legs to her chest and buried her face in her crossed arms. She was uninjured, save a bruised rear end and a throbbing toe, but her mind was spinning in chaotic, unpredictable circles.

This can't be real.

Places like this don't exist Helen, don't be stupid.

This is you unmedicated, Helen, just like it always is.

You should've listened to your mother-

"Helen? Helen!"

Luciana's hurried footsteps couldn't penetrate the fog of Helen's mind, but the warmth of her arms, as her host embraced her, did. The taller woman's arms were comforting and strong, wrapping her all the way around as she sat beside her on the tile floor.

"Helen, I'm so sorry, I don't understand what happened I-I just thought maybe we could see more of the grounds and I-"

"Are you real?"

"Am I... real, I don't understand-"

"I just need to hear you say that you're real, please."

Perhaps it was the desperation in Helen's voice, perhaps it was the tears in her eyes, but Luciana's concern turned to sadness.

"Helen, I'm *real*," the woman said fiercely, pulling her arms back and putting a hand on either side of Helen's face. "I *am* real, and you *are* safe."

Helen blinked in surprise as Luciana pulled her closer and kissed her deeply. This was not the wild, reckless meeting of lips from the morning, but rather the deeper passion of a deliberate and intimate act.

When their lips finally parted, Helen gasped for air, left breathless by Luciana's sudden absence.

"I'm sorry-"

Luciana held a finger to her still wet lips and shook her head, holding out Helen's glasses in her other hand..

"You have nothing to be sorry for. You're *human*, Helen, and all that that entails. Don't apologize for being you."

Helen opened her mouth to speak again but was cut off once more.

"And before you say anything silly about 'owing me,' remember what I said before."

"There is no debt," Helen repeated in a faux ominous tone, rolling her eyes with a gentle smile.

"That's right," Luciana kissed her cheek and moved to stand. "There is no debt."

Helen studied the taller woman, now standing over her with her hand held out. She knew she was prone to launching herself into things, and that her feelings often ruled her decisions, but the pull this woman had on her was... she struggled for an adequate comparison.

Luciana was the Earth, and Helen, the moon caught helplessly in her orbit.

"Penny for your thoughts?"

"Nothing I just...," Helen let Luciana help her to her feet. "You're... Well, things like this don't happen. Not to me."

"I'm no fairy tale, Helen," Luciana's smile faltered. "If I was, I wouldn't be all alone, right?"

Luciana turned back to the door, her hand still firmly holding Helen's, but Helen stood her ground.

"So you are alone here? Just you and Armand in this giant place?"

"Yes," Luciana looked back over her shoulder at her. "And we have been for a very long time."

"Don't you get lonely?"

"Every day."

Helen wondered if the moisture in Luciana's eyes was real or imagined, but the strain in the woman's voice told her plenty. She felt the pressure on her hand start to ease and, fearing Luciana might let go, she took a step forward and allowed herself to be led back to the entryway.

"So," Luciana winked, her casual carefree demeanor returned. "Where were we?"

"Right," Helen smiled back timidly. "I'm not sure, you were going to- whoa!"

Luciana broke out into wild laughter as she pulled Helen down the hall and out into the rain, twirling her around and catching her in what could only be described as ballroom dance.

Cold rain and warm hands caught Helen's nerves on fire and she found herself face to face with her host, one hand joined with hers and the other resting gently on her shoulder. Luciana's empty hand drifted down to Helen's hip and her eyes locked on to Helen's with a ferocity.

Helen blinked water out of her eyes, feeling an electric tingle with every drop of rain running down her face, her neck, her arms, and legs. The loose silk kimono she wore clung to her as it was slowly soaked with rainwater, and Helen couldn't help but notice that Luciana's was similarly clinging to her powerful frame.

"W-we're going to ruin your kimonos," she breathed.

"They're just clothes," Luciana took a step forward and Helen's body responded automatically. "Memories are priceless."

Helen allowed Luciana to lead her across the flagstones of the courtyard, trusting her direction instinctively. She clung to Luciana's hand as she swung about, twirling across the stone with absolute confidence that her partner wouldn't let her fall. She had the passing desire to look at her surroundings, but she couldn't tear her eyes away from Luciana's, and she knew that nothing around her would match them for beauty and depth.

Helen gasped and clung tightly to Luciana as they stopped suddenly, Helen leaning back until her hair almost brushed the stones, and Luciana's firm arms supporting her. Both women were breathing heavily and Helen found herself copying Luciana's bright smile.

"You dance spectacularly," Luciana announced, lifting Helen back into a standing position.

"I dance terribly," Helen laughed. "And I have certainly never danced like *that* before. That was all you-"

"You must have trusted me quite a lot then, for that to go so smoothly?"

"I do," Helen blurted out, turning red. "I do trust you, um, a lot."

"I, ah," Luciana blinked rapidly and shook her head. "I'm so sorry I can't stay longer."

"But-"

"I have to do a little... work," Luciana released Helen's hands and stepped back. "In my office. Upstairs. Please, feel free to explore the grounds."

"Wait," Helen replayed the last few moments, looking for a reason for the sudden change in mood. "Did I do something wrong?"

"No," Luciana replied fervently. "No, you didn't. I just realized there was something I needed to do, that's all. Please, I could have Armand bring you an umbrella-"

"No, I er, I would rather feel the rain I think, if it's all the same."

Luciana turned to walk away but glanced back over her shoulder.

"This was fun, *really* fun. I'll be back soon and we'll do lunch, alright?"

Helen watched her host disappear into the house and felt her shoulders slump.

What did you do now?

Already soaking wet, Helen didn't mind the rain. In fact, she'd spent many a day wandering in rainstorms just like this one when she was a child. It was so peaceful, so raw, and it almost guaranteed she'd be alone.

With no particular direction in mind, she took a better look at her surroundings. The house was formidable. From her place just outside the awning, she saw that it was backed all the way against the cliff towering above it. Turning, she could see there was no lawn, per se, but rather a sort of semi-maintained wildlife sanctuary consisting of an expanse of native flowers, bushes, and grasses, as well as bird feeders, bat houses, and a few large fruit trees.

Not wishing to walk through the plants, she followed a path of crushed rock that served as a driveway. It was narrow, barely wide enough for a car and a half, and it wound through the plant life for a hundred feet or so before it straightened out and opened into a small plaza.

Reaching the plaza, she found a wide fountain. It was manmade, but the smooth stonework was organic and raw. Helen could see golden koi swimming through lilies, their reflections muddled by the ripples from the rain. She didn't stop for long though, something was tugging her onward. She peered through the rain and noted with curiosity that there was a wall just past a small stretch of grass beyond the fountain. She stepped toward it and felt a sort of electric charge building within her - not unlike the feeling she'd had with Luciana when she first came outside.

Helen resisted the urge to turn back and continued forward, her brow wrinkling as she realized the wall she was approaching was, in fact, a towering set of rose bushes stretching off out of sight in either direction. She came to a halt a few feet from the wall of greenery to marvel at the fist sized blossoms that adorned the bush. They seemed impervious to the rain, and not a single petal was out of place despite the storms of the past few days.

The flowers were not the only oversized feature of the plants, their thorns were an inch or more in length and visibly razor sharp. This, combined with the fact that the wall was at least eight feet tall, told her the bushes must be ancient.

"Jesus," she mumbled to no one in particular. "What is she feeding these things?"

The wall had no visible means to pass through it - at least not right here - so she resolved to follow the curious feature.

Five minutes of walking brought her up against the cliff wall once more. She could see the house, maybe a stone's throw away across a patch of wildflowers, and was surprised she'd missed the wall earlier.

She chewed her lip and narrowed her eyes, before concluding that perhaps the original tennant had designed the rose bushes as a sort of wall or privacy fence.

Still, there had to be an entrance *somewhere*.

Helen pulled her kimono more tightly around herself and headed back in the opposite direction. She was quite used to walking barefoot, and relished the feelings of soft grasses and smooth stones.

She was nearly convinced the hedge had no opening when out of the gloom a wide stone arch appeared. She realized quickly that if she'd simply followed the original path of crushed rock it would have taken her directly here, and kicked herself for not considering that the driveway would obviously lead out of the property. She stepped out of the grass and onto the pathway, turning to face the broad entrance.

The archway was made of massive stacked stones and was completely overgrown with roses and mosses. Flowering stalks traveled unbroken from one side of the gate to the other, and then reformed a hedge wall and continued on into the rain.

The path pushed outward about fifty paces before it met a river - no doubt the river that Helen had plunged into just a few days ago.

Helen suppressed a shiver as she observed the still swollen water rushing across her field of vision. She could see the ruined remains of a low wooden bridge - as evidenced by cracked pillars at either side of the river, and some dense foliage on the other side. Large rocks dotted the banks and - Her jaw popped open as she registered the fact that *one* of those rocks was in fact the crumpled remains of her slate gray sedan.

The front windshield was almost entirely missing, and the driver's side window had a spiderweb crack in the middle. In fact, the car was folded nearly in half, and the entire front end was crumpled. It resembled a beer can that had been crushed against some frat boy's head, and then tossed carelessly aside.

She started forward, instinctively moving towards her vehicle to inspect the damage. She made it to the very edge of the arch when she froze, her foot hovering mid-step. The charge she'd been feeling intensified and she felt herself compelled to take a step backwards. Helen shook her head, and tried to step forward once again, only to find herself turning back up the path.

A sudden, strong sense of doubt entered her mind.

What use was there in going to see the car? The thing was trashed, there wasn't going to be anything useful in there, and she was just as likely to get hurt trying to investigate. No, it was better to leave it be, at least until the storms were past.

Turning from the path once more, she headed further along the hedge hoping eventually to find either another way out or where it connected with the cliffs behind the manor.

Twenty minutes later - at least by her reckoning - she came to a stop. The hedge continued with only a gentle curve as far as she could see.

She was surrounded here by boulders ranging in size from a suitcase to a small car, all old enough to have a heavy coating of moss upon their stoney faces.

Beyond and between the stones she could see a fairly dense patch of trees. The wide boles made it challenging to determine just how deep the stand of trees was, and whether it was part of a larger forest or not.

How big is this place?

Helen sat gingerly upon the nearest rock of reasonable size, pulling at the kimono to secure it underneath her, and took stock. Although she couldn't see any part of the mansion at this point, knowing she could follow the hedge back gave her plenty of peace of mind. That said, she hadn't the foggiest idea of how far the hedge ran or whether any of the territory was dangerous. Even if there weren't any wildlife, what would happen should she turn her ankle, break a leg, or worse?

She felt her chest tighten and her breath start to stutter as she was unwillingly dragged into a spiral of anxious thoughts and terrible what-ifs.

Get ahold of yourself, Helen...

A bolt of lighting and the crackling bang of accompanying thunder shook the skies and Helen flinched as though she'd be struck.

She glanced skyward in time to get hit in the face with the first drops of a sudden downpour that drove her into the shelter of the nearest tree.

"Dammit, Helen," she clenched her jaw and slogged further into the trees. "How stupid are you? Wandering off, not knowing the area. Now your stupid ass is-"

The harsh caw of a crow ripped her attention skyward once more. By the sounds of it, the bird had to be huge, or at least-

Helen caught sight of the bird immediately, it was massive, its oil-slick darkness contrasting against the cloudy gray skies, and the dark browns and greens of the forest.

The creature tilted its head, regarding her with wide, intelligent eyes.

"What?" Helen shouted after a moment of silence. "What are you looking at, huh?"

The bird puffed up its feathers and loudly cawed again, this time with an unmistakably angry tone. Helen took a step back and felt some of the color drain from her face as first one, then three more crows landed in the branches above her.

"What the hell?"

The chorus of screams from the birds was deafening, and despite Helen putting her hands over her ears, she could barely hear herself think.

"Alright already," she shouted, throwing her hands up. "I'm sorry I yelled at you!"

An eerie silence fell immediately, and Helen shrank beneath the judgemental gaze of the ominous flock.

"I'm sorry, I'm having a… Well, I'm having a *moment* and I shouldn't have… I don't know."

Her voice trailed off and her gaze dropped to the forest floor.

What are you doing, Helen? Talking to birds?

A flutter of feathers startled her enough to duck as the birds above her took off en masse.

All save the largest one, the one she'd first encountered.

This enormous creature fluttered down to ground level, landing delicately on a large rock perhaps ten feet away.

"You're a very odd creature," Helen addressed the bird with wary politeness. "Beautiful, but - oh!"

The bird hopped to a closer stone, and then hopped closer still, landing eye level with her, just out of arm's reach.

"You're a bit, uh, scary," she backed away slowly. "Am I near your nest or? I can leave you, I don't mind at all..."

Her short, nervous footsteps were taking her backwards deeper into the woods and away from the hedgerow.

For some reason, the crow seemed *more* agitated as she backed away, but it didn't appear to desire to draw any closer to her. Instead, it was giving out short, frustrated squawks and flapping its wings at her.

"Nice and easy," Helen tried to channel peace and tranquility. "Nice birdie."

She turned her head, trying to get a quick glance behind herself and ensure she wouldn't trip.

It looked like there was a little clearing just behind her.

"Stahp!"

Helen snapped back forward, her left foot hovering in mid-air, and locked eyes with the crow, which was leaning forward awkwardly with its wings out.

"D-did you just *talk*?"

The crow settled itself and eyed her quizzically, but said nothing.

Birds don't talk, Helen, don't be stupid.

"Parrots do," she mumbled to herself as she put her foot down. She turned her attention back to the bird. "You did talk, right?"

The crow squawked and hopped backwards as she took a step forward.

"Why'd you stop me?" she brushed rain-slick hair back over her ear and turned around to look back where she'd been headed.

She was about two feet from the edge of a perfectly circular clearing of bright green grass and wildflowers, with nothing untoward about it.

"There's nothing here, bird," she rolled her eyes and took a small step towards the circle just as a cloudbreak sent a ray of light shining down upon it. "Just a gorgeous glade and warm sunshine."

She felt a tug in the back of her mind, telling her to go back to the mansion and to forget this place, but another more visceral tug pulled at her heart and told her to move closer, to revel in the wonder of the delicate flowers and soft grass and - mushrooms?

The sunlight glinted off the bright white stalks and muddy brown caps of a patch of mushrooms beside her feet. Suddenly she realized the whole of the circle was ringed with patches of the fungi, which under the gloomy skies had blended so perfectly with the wet ground.

"Oh you're a superstitious old bird," she joked, turning around to find that the crow was nowhere to be seen.

Another boom of thunder overhead told her that contemplating the unusual behavior of the local birds could wait until she was inside - inside and dried off. A steep breeze rifled through the trees and Helen realized how chilled she'd become, her hands had a purplish tint and no doubt her lips were blue as well.

Her thoughts turned to hot coffee and the large fireplace in the library, and she let her feet carry her back toward the hedge. The trip there took longer than she thought it ought to, she must've been deeper into the woods than she'd thought.

Soon enough, however, the wall of thorns and blossoms loomed ahead of her. She took a sharp right turn and headed off down the hedge at a brisk walk, hoping to work some warmth back into her limbs as she went.

Some time later, when the manor finally loomed large and she'd returned to the crushed gravel path that she now knew led to the door, she let out the sigh of relief she'd been holding in.

The house *was* real, and that meant she was safe.

She started off down the path then paused.

"It'd be nice to bring a few flowers back for the table," she considered aloud. "Or maybe just one, for Luciana."

The thought of her intriguing host brought a flood of memories of their morning and, despite the chill in the air, Helen's cheeks burned.

Her course decided, she returned to the hedgerow and delicately plucked one of the massive blossoms, as well as about six inches of the stem. The flower gave way with a snap, and Helen brought it to her nose to enjoy the heady, rich scent of it.

A soft crackling sound drew her eyes back to the hedgerow where she was alarmed to see that the area she'd plucked the flower from was now black, shriveled, and dead.

"Fuck," she drew closer. "God dammit, Helen, you idiot."

Kill your host's flowers? Classic, Helen.

The blighted area spread before her eyes until it covered an area about the size of a volleyball, and then stopped. Helen waited a moment, expecting the worst, but the bush appeared to have stabilized. She shut her eyes and shook her head.

That wasn't real, that was-

She peeked an eye open and was relieved to find the massive dead spot was gone, and that the only sign of her pulling out the rose was an ugly blackish-purple patch of the hedgerow the size of her palm.

Perhaps, she reassured herself, this variety of roses simply bruises extremely easily? Determined not to do any more damage, she headed back up the path and made a beeline for the door.

Chapter Six

"Welcome back, ma'am."

As the door opened at her approach, Helen found she was no longer surprised by Armand's near-psychic anticipation of her movements, rather she was grateful for the pair of fluffy pink towels he had draped over his arm.

"Lady De la Rosa is preparing lunch, and I have drawn a bath for you in the master suite, should you require it."

Lunch? Didn't we just eat breakfast?

Helen considered posing the question, but second-guessed herself almost immediately.

"Thank you, Armand," she answered warmly, hoping to break past his impeccably stoic exterior. "You are very kind."

For his part, Armand simply gave a short bow, shut the door behind her, and then walked away.

"Right," Helen mumbled, toweling herself off as best she could in the tiled entryway.

A warm bath did sound inviting - hell, it sounded *divine* - but Helen found herself turning toward the kitchen, rather than the stairway. She made her way through the library, down the warm, silent halls of the estate until she reached the dining room. By now she could smell fragrant spices and the unmistakable scent of roasting meat.

She took a deep breath, inhaling tantalizing hints of cumin, mint, and lemon, as well as the sharp heat of chiles. The combination had her mouth watering even before she pushed open the door to the dining room. She was more than a little surprised when her stomach growled - normally she was a fairly light eater, and she wasn't prone to snacking.

Entering the dining space, she took stock. As before, there were only two place settings - both down at the end - but it wasn't the cutlery or even the room itself that captured Helen's attention. She cocked her head to the side and listened. Amidst the soft clink of cooking implements coming from the next room, she could faintly hear *singing*.

She broke into a smile and closed her eyes, losing herself in the brassy tones of the woman's soulful voice. She didn't know the song, and she hadn't the faintest clue what language the lyrics were, but the melody was low, slow, and mournful.

Minutes passed in relative quiet while Helen hovered between interrupting and simply enjoying the impromptu concert. Luciana crooned away, seamlessly blending languages, tone, and tenor as she sang with the confidence of an unwatched performer.

Finally, Helen decided that she should intrude upon her host rather than listen on, reasoning that perhaps it was unfair that Luciana didn't know she was listening. She set the broad rose upon the table and, in a fit of impish delight, stripped out of her still-damp kimono and wrapped herself scantily in a single towel. The fluffy garment barely extended a few inches past her hips, and left the bulk of her breasts exposed as well.

After taking a moment to make sure the top of the towel was tight - and therefore presenting her chest in the best possible way - she tiptoed to the door and gently pushed it open.

Nothing could have prepared Helen for what she saw as she slipped into the kitchen.

She stood frozen, eyes wide and jaw slack as she took in the scene. Luciana, clad in a sapphire sundress, was dancing lighty around the far end of the kitchen. Her hands, which were both outstretched, were both engulfed in globes of deep violet light that crackled internally with lightning every few seconds.

She was surrounded by a rotating ring of floating, fiery-orange symbols that looked as though they had been carved into the air itself, and different objects all over the kitchen were *moving*.

Pots and pans were bouncing in and out of a sink full of soapy water, scrubbed by a brush that was moving by itself in midair, a mop was wiping away some unseen spot in the far corner, and cabinets were opening by themselves as bottles of liquid and canisters of dried spices floated down toward the counter-top.

The stove, which looked once more like an ancient, cast iron behemoth and not a beautiful modern appliance, had two skillets and a pot all set over different burners, each stirred, unmanned by long-handled wooden spoons

Helen tried desperately to make sense of the scene before her eyes, but all she could think was that it had finally happened, she'd finally hit the point in her lack of medication that reality started to remold itself. She pinched herself hard, hard enough that she'd likely have a bruise, and scrunched her eyes shut.

It's bullshit. None of it is real, Helen, just take a breath.

Her eyes were shut so tight that it hurt, and her fingernails dug into her palms as she counted, clearing her mind of anything else.

One one-thousand, two one-thousand, three one-thousand, four one-thousand, five one-thousand. Ok Helen, everything is going to be back to normal-

She cracked an eyelid, then snapped both eyes back open. Nothing had changed, the impossible was still occurring right before her eyes.

"Fuck me," she marvelled. "It's not possible-"

Her voice, though low, was loud enough to alert her host.

Luciana spun in an instant, freezing with both hands still in the air and the same look on her face that a deer has in front of an oncoming truck.

For a moment all of time and space stood still. The sponges, spoons, pots, and pans all froze mid-motion, Luciana and Helen were unmoving and unblinking in the most unexpected staring contest, and all the sounds that had filled the kitchen moments before abruptly halted.

"Oh!"

Luciana's single word, uttered out of a mixture of shock and embarrassment, broke the veil that hung over the room. Her hands stopped glowing instantaneously; all of the dirty dishes in the sink splashed into the soapy water, sponges landing on them gracelessly; pots and pans settled with a clatter on a shiny new stainless steel stove; and all of the spinning, glowing symbols surrounding the woman blinked out of existence with a sharp, short-lived sizzle.

"Oh? *Oh*? Are you serious?" Helen shook her head, never breaking eye contact with Luciana. "That's it, just 'oh?'"

"Helen, I'm, well I'm not sure what to say," Luciana held her hands out, attempting to placate her guest in the way one might react to a violent criminal. "I can explain, but I need you to be *calm*, and to-"

"Oh my god," Helen put a hand to her head and started pacing. "Y-you need me to be calm? I am *freaking out* right now Luciana. I, just... well, I mean what the-"

"Helen," Luciana's voice was forceful but soft, pouring over her like raw honey. "Please, it's going to be ok."

"Ok, ok," Helen stopped pacing for a moment, only to immediately resume. "I'm calm. I'm uh, I'm listening."

"Alright," Luciana sighed with obvious relief. "But you're going to want to sit down."

The woman snapped her fingers and gestured at Helen, who jumped back in surprise upon seeing a comfortable looking wooden chair just behind her, perfectly positioned.

"Ok, that has to stop," she pointed in disbelief at the errant furniture. "That has to stop until I figure out what is happening and if *any* of this is real."

"Don't worry, I'm real. It's all real," Luciana seemed to hesitate before continuing. "That's actually going to be the *easy* part to believe."

"I…" Helen cut herself off, simply staring for fear of what she might say.

Or you're in a padded room, that's easy enough to believe.

"Helen?"

"Just… just start at the beginning."

"Ok, the beginning." Luciana paused, then seemed to settle on a place to start. "Well, there are actually *several* paths to magic, why don't we start there?"

Half an hour later, Luciana was leaning against the counter, her arms crossed and a crooked half smile gracing her lips, while Helen was fairly glued to the chair - which was the only thing keeping her from falling over from shock.

"Ok, let me get this straight," Helen took a deep breath. "I'm not hallucinating. This is totally, really happening. You're a... wizard? You're *not* human. And, naturally, you do real, no-bullshit magic?"

"That's... correct," Luciana uncrossed her arms. "For the most part. I'm a witch, not a wizard and-"

"Right, sorry."

"No problem," she continued, waving Helen's apology aside. "And yes, I do a little magic here and there - nothing earth-shattering - and... no, I'm not, strictly speaking, human."

"Ok, not strictly speaking meaning what, in this context?"

"There are disagreements about the origins of Fae and our connection with humanity," Luciana chewed her lip. "Some argue that we have common ancestry, but the prevailing theory is convergent coevolution."

Helen ran her fingers through her still-wet hair and tried to stop the reeling in her mind. She watched as Luciana's face slowly filled with concern while the silence between them grew.

"Helen I *know* this feels big…"

"*Feels*?" Helen squeaked.

"It feels like this world-changing thing," she continued. "But it's not, nothing has-"

"How can you say that?" Helen gulped air like a fish out of water, fighting hyperventilation. "How can you say nothing has changed?"

"Because, Helen," Luciana walked over and crouched down beside her, bringing their eyes level once more. "This world already existed just as it does right now, you've simply found a clearer view of it."

"Ok, um," Luciana's voice went a long way towards soothing her. "Well, what now?"

"I think that depends on you?"

Though her words were the same, Luciana's posture was much different than it had been when she'd uttered those words to Helen just a few hours past. The confident, hungry woman who had pinned her to the wall in her walk-in closet was more reserved now, cautious even. Luciana scanned her eyes with a palpable intensity that left Helen breathless.

"What's for lunch?"

Helen's question was perfectly accompanied by a sudden, drawn-out gurgle from her stomach that sparked a cautious smile on Luciana's face.

"I suppose you *must* be hungry, for as long as you spent out there."

"Ah yes, an hour or so of walking is good for the appetite," Helen smiled back, patting her stomach with faux sincerity.

"Er," Luciana faltered. "Did you go into the woods, by chance?"

"I did...."

"Ah," Luciana's cheeks reddened. "I didn't think you'd go that far."

"I don't understand."

"It's actually been about *five* hours," she flashed a shaky smile.

Helen's mouth worked but no words came out.

"The woods are enchanted-"

"Enchanted," she found her voice as suddenly as she'd lost it. "What the hell does that mean, enchant- Hey! If I've been gone for five freaking hours, why didn't you come look for me!?"

"Helen," Luciana was suddenly serious. "I *swear* to you, as long as I am here these grounds are safe for you. Always."

The raw power in the woman's voice sent a tingle down Helen's spine - and elsewhere. Helen was acutely aware of the nearness of her host once more, and that in her crouched position Helen could see almost all of the way down her-

"See something you like?" Luciana smirked, drawing Helen's guilty attention back to her face.

"I do," Helen cracked a smile as well. "Sorry."

"Lunch first," Luciana stood and headed back towards the stove. "Sexy things later."

"Yes ma'am," Helen answered playfully as Luciana neared the stove.

Luciana froze mid-step and turned to look back at her with one eyebrow quirked.

"What?"

Luciana flicked her wrist, igniting a halo of golden light around her hand. The aura swayed and flowed like flames, and was shot through with swirling silver sparks. Helen's eyes went wide and she felt glued to her seat at the display. Behind her host, the shiny new stove reverted once more to a massive iron beast straight from the 19th century.

"That's, that's amazing-"

Helen squeaked as the chair she sat in began to glide swiftly and silently across the kitchen floor. She pressed back against the chair and held on with an iron grip as she closed the distance to Luciana in a fraction of a second.

"Did you just call me *ma'am*," Luciana questioned, leaning in close.

"I-I-I was just-"

"Hands on the armrests," Luciana ordered, her voice like a whip wrapped in velvet.

Helen complied instantly, her heart hitching in her chest and her mind racing. The strength, the *authority* that rolled off her host in waves was igniting a fire in her that demanded attention.

Luciana snapped her fingers again and silk ropes slithered out from the armrests of the chair, binding Helen's arms firmly but painlessly in place. Helen's blood pressure spiked and her eyes zeroed in on Luciana's. Her heart was throbbing in her chest, her ears, and between her thighs as well. She squirmed, rubbing her thighs together and clenching and releasing her fists.

"Comfortable?"

"A-actually," Helen bit her lip, then took the dive. "They could be a little, um, tighter?"

Luciana's eyebrows shot up for a moment, but she obligingly held her glowing hand out, curling her fingers in a fairly suggestive way, and slowly twisted her hand clockwise. As she did so, the silver sparks pulsed within and Helen could immediately feel the ropes begin to cinch tighter.

"Say when."

"Yes ma'am," Helen closed her eyes and held her tongue until the ropes were painful, but not overwhelming.

"There, please," Helen was doing her best not to pant.

The ropes stopped tightening and Helen opened her eyes again. Luciana was standing about three feet away, closer to the stove, and all of the pots, pans, and implements were back at their work - diligently cooking and cleaning away around them.

"Is it warm in this kitchen?"

Helen mulled over Luciana's question, it *felt* like a trap somehow. She didn't have much experience doing this, but what little she did suggested that…

"Yes, it's hot."

Luciana tilted her head and Helen felt the ropes start to loosen. Helen pouted, moaning with disappointment as the stimulation ended unexpectedly.

"It's hot…," Luciana looked on expectantly.

"It's hot, *ma'am*," Helen corrected.

She let out an unconscious moan of pleasure as the ropes pulled taut again.

"We don't have to do this, to play this game," Luciana pointed out, her voice soft and kind once more. "Unless… you want to?"

"Yes ma'am," Helen nodded fervently. "Please?"

"My pleasure," Luciana smiled wickedly.

The woman stood up, towering over Helen, then backed away toward the stove. She moved fluidly, as gracefully as a cat and as captivating as slow-poured honey.

"So," Luciana reached for the thin silk ribbon holding her robe closed, toying with the knot. "I believe you asked what was for lunch?"

Helen was too enraptured by Luciana's hands to realize she'd been asked a question, and it wasn't until her chin was firmly dragged upward by a cool, unyielding force that she met Luciana's eyes again. Her eyes widened upon noticing that Luciana was several feet away. The woman's eyebrow was arched, and she had a devious grin on her face.

"Not paying attention?"

"Sorry ma'am," Helen managed, gasping a little as the force held her chin in place. "H-how're you doing that?"

Luciana's laughter was like the sparkle in a fountain on a sunny day, and Helen felt the force subside until she was free to move her head again.

"*Magic*, Helen," Luciana approached again, untying the knot in her hands with painstaking slowness.

She paused less than a foot in front of Helen, so close and yet just beyond Helen's reach. Helen struggled in vain against the cords around her wrists while Luciana pulled the ribbon free at last. The thin silk robe opened just enough to show Luciana's deep cleavage, her delicate collarbones, and her bare skin all the way down to her thighs, which were held just *so*, in a way that prevented Helen from seeing what she wanted.

Helen's mouth watered and she tried to swallow the lump in her throat. She tore her eyes away from the center of her desire and looked up to Luciana's striking face.

"Such restraint," Luciana purred. "But let's remove temptation."

Luciana took the ribbon that she still held in her hands and deftly secured it around Helen's head, blindfolding her with frustrating thoroughness. Helen couldn't see the faintest spec of light around the thin fabric, but as seconds ticked by her every sense became more and more magnified. She could feel the lightest stirring of air brushing against her skin, raising goosebumps across her body. She could feel the soft silken threads of the kimono brushing against her thighs, crumpled behind her back, and resting gently on her full, raised nipples. The grain of the wood under her arms, the exquisite chill of the tile below her feet, and the smells and sounds of the kitchen at work.

"You are so beautiful."

Helen jumped, half due to Luciana's soft voice and half from the electrifying sensation of her fingers brushing along Helen's jawline.

"S-so, what now, ma'am?"

"Well," Luciana kissed Helen's cheek, then down to the side of her neck. "We need to get you fed."

Helen shivered as Luciana's warm, talented mouth worked its way across to her collarbone and then down to the top of her breast.

"Right?"

"Mhmm," was all Helen could manage, she was already trembling with desire.

"How about an appetizer, and perhaps a game?"

"A game, ma'am?"

"Yes, open wide."

Helen complied instantly, feeling only the slightest bit silly.

"Here's a sweet treat," Luciana whispered. "Tell me what it is."

Helen felt something cool and fairly smooth rub gently across her bottom lip. She tilted her head forward and took a timid bite. The item was soft, juicy, and exploding with a delicious and immediately recognizable flavor.

"Strawberry," Helen giggled.

"Very good."

Helen had to struggle to swallow as she felt one of Luciana's hands slide down between her clenched thighs. Her legs sprung open immediately, almost begging for Luciana to explore her. Luciana's strong fingers worked inward until they came to a pause scant centimeters from her outer lips.

"Hmm," Luciana rubbed slow circles in the moisture on Helen's inner thighs. "You *are* hungry. Let's try a harder one."

Helen opened her mouth expectantly.

This time, there were a variety of textures and flavors. Whatever it was, was cool and crunchy, on the outside, savory, warm, and tender on the inside, and all dressed with some kind of tangy sauce and a mild, firm... cheese?

"Well?"

Helen tried to concentrate, but Luciana's hand was sliding closer, until her fingertips brushed the lips between her legs.

"I-I'm not sure," Helen chewed on, then swallowed. "I think lettuce, wrapped around... steak? Maybe? With like asiago and some kind of-"

"Carpaccio," Luciana's smile was easy to hear. "It's called carpaccio, and yes, you're absolutely correct."

Helen whimpered as Luciana's hand moved to engulf her vulva entirely, her middle and ring fingers slipping between her lips and playing delicately in the wetness they discovered.

"P-please," she huffed, breathing hard.

"Not yet," Luciana teased. "We've another round to go before dessert."

Helen pouted, but, if Luciana noticed, she didn't say anything.

"Alright, here we go…"

Helen opened her mouth again. This was another multi-faceted treat. The bottom layer was easy to pick out - it was some kind of toasted bread - but above that was the most marvelously warm, rich, and creamy substance, all mixed up with what had to be cool blackberry jam.

"Oh my god," Helen muttered past a mouth full of food. "That's *amazing!*"

"Isn't it?" Luciana breathed, her fingers slowly working their way deeper. "Crostada with brie and blackberry jam."

Helen shivered, her toes curling unconsciously as she felt Luciana's fingers curl upward inside her. Her gasp of pleasure turned to a shudder of ecstasy as she felt Luciana's thumb gently press against her clitoris.

"I believe some mention was made of dessert," Luciana mumbled, her lips pressed against Helen's neck in a lingering kiss.

"Y-yes," Helen was straining against the ropes holding her arms to no avail, and she was certain her nails were digging into the wooden armrests with enough force to mar the surface.

Helen blinked back tears as the blindfold was unexpectedly removed. The silk ribbon fell to her shoulders as her blurred vision came into focus.

Luciana barely gave her time to think though, moving her lips from Helen's neck to her mouth and leaning hard into a passionate play of tongues.

When Luciana withdrew at last, they were both panting for air and grinning wildly.

"Are you... ready for dessert?"

Helen nodded fervently.

"Are you sure? You don't even know what it-"

"I want it," Helen blurted out recklessly.

"So sure of yourself," Luciana teased wickedly.

Helen felt her lover's fingers slowly slide out from between her lips and felt a sudden emptiness that made her ache all the more.

"Wait, what're you doing?"

"Such a *look*," Luciana teased.

But rather than return, Luciana stood and backed away. She slipped out of the kimono and snapped her fingers, sitting down heavily onto a plump cushioned chair that appeared beneath her.

Helen drank in the sight of the woman as she reclined. Her body was bathed in soft light and her scarred, smooth skin tugged at Helen's stomach. Luciana leaned back, throwing one leg over the armrest of the chair and giving Helen a full view of her own visibly wet sex.

"Luciana," Helen breathed, her heart skipping a beat.

"Afraid I'll leave you out?"

"A little," Helen murmured nervously. "I think I'd go insane-"

Helen stutterred to a stop as Luciana drew her long slender fingers across the orb of her breast, ending with a flourish around her nipple. The sight alone was maddening, but Helen *felt* it, felt it as clearly as if it had been her own breast under Luciana's fingers.

"Ah, *now* you understand," Luciana's grin was wide and the glint in her eyes was mesmerizing.

One hand still gently toying with her breast, Luciana took her other hand - the one she'd been fingering Helen with moments before - and brought her still slick fingers to her mouth. She swirled her tongue across the digits in lazy spirals, and in return Helen could feel that probing tongue swirling across her clitoris and between her lips. She struggled hard to keep from crying out with pleasure, and was soon convulsing and biting her lip hard enough to taste blood.

The torturous rapture ended as quickly as it had begun though, and her vision snapped back to Luciana. The woman was slowly snaking her hand down her chest, across her belly, and between her thighs. Helen felt those strong fingers as they gently traced the outside of her lips, then cried out as Luciana plunged inside her.

Luciana worked a different kind of magic between her lips and inside of her, and Helen lost count of the number of times she was brought to a peak, only to plunge deeper into pleasure on the other side. Time lost meaning while Luciana pleasured herself just a foot or so away, her orgasms mirroring Helen's as the women drowned in each other's pleasure.

When Luciana subsided at last, they were both breathless, with sweaty brows and abs sore from convulsions.

"Holy shit," Helen managed. "That was… that was incredible."

"Would it be too 'on the nose,'" Luciana struggled to sit up. "to say 'my pleasure?'"

Chapter Seven

"C7 to C5."

Luciana chewed her fingernail as the small stone emblem slid across the library floor, then glanced up at Helen.

"Traditional response to E4, I suppose," her eyes narrowed. "You mentioned you play?"

"A little," Helen grinned back at her host.

"So then it's no coincidence, you playing the-"

"Sicilian Defense? No, not a coincidence."

"Hmm," Luciana sighed. "I should've known not to believe you. *Nobody* who says they play 'a little' is being honest."

"Methinks the lady doth protest too much," Helen grinned. "Besides, the offer was too tempting to resist, no?"

"Unfortunately, *most* bets are too tempting to resist," Luciana sighed. "Especially when betting on the outcome of a game."

"What do you mean?"

"It's a trait we Fae share. We love puzzles, riddles, tricks, and gambling of any kind."

"Fae?"

Helen studied her host, who for all the world appeared fully human. She had no pointed ears, nor wings or fangs or horns or any other traits that she would associate with the supernatural - and yet she had no reason to doubt the woman's words.

"Fae is a collective term; it encompasses all that our species represents."

"So are there other supernatural creatures then, vampires and werewolves and-"

"We Fae believe that to speak of a thing is to draw its attention, Helen, so we tend to stray away from mentioning certain iterations of our kind."

"Ah, I-I-I'm sorry I-"

"You couldn't have known," Luciana waved away her apology. "To answer your question, yes… and no."

"Mmm," Helen rolled her eyes. "I'm picking up on the riddles thing, and don't forget it's still your move."

"Right right, B1 to C3," Luciana had a fierce determination in her eyes, which she had yet to take off the chessboard. "And all of those things you mentioned, as well as a great many others, are all the same species."

"I don't understand."

"It's...," she sighed heavily. "All Fae have been born and reborn a thousand times, since the dawn of time. We do not age beyond adulthood, we do not grow sick, and though we *can* be killed, we rarely are. Instead, as a Fae passes through time we grow in power-"

"You grow in power?"

"I'm explaining this poorly," Luciana rubbed her temples. "Fae are a... closed system. There exists only so much Fae energy, and it is tied up in the lifeforce of every living Fae. A Fae child cannot be born unless another Fae perishes or the parents willingly sacrifice some of their own energy. Fae who exist for long enough collect some of the energy that sheds off when others die, and so the longer a Fae persists, the more powerful they become."

"That doesn't explain how all of those creatures are the same species though, D7 to D6."

"As a Fae accumulates power, they can *transform* after a fashion, like a snake shedding its skin. We are born small, fairly weak, and in the form of gnomes or brownies and the like. With power, we grow, and as we outgrow our previous forms, we transition to larger and more powerful ones."

"Well, how do you look human and others are… well monsters?"

"We have more and more control over it as we grow," Luciana suddenly seemed a bit… cagey. "We can… choose our path. When we are powerful enough, we can even choose to adopt only certain traits of a chosen form, if we want."

"Right, so dragons then, Fae?"

"Yes."

"Trolls?"

"Mhmm."

"What about dwarves? Elves? Goblin-"

"Yes," Luciana laughed brightly. "Yes, all the various creatures from your myths and legends are actually just shades of Fae."

"And you sort of fade back into some bigger energy pool and that's why there's no bones or anything?"

"Correct."

"So why aren't there any more?"

"More what, dragons?"

"Yes, and all the rest. If you've been around forever then why not pick the biggest and most powerful form?"

"Power and size are not necessarily linked," Luciana smiled. "It's also a fair sight easier not to get murdered by knights in shining armor if you're not a giant fire-breathing behemoth."

"So then what kind of Fae are you? What have you been?"

Luciana jerked her head up at the question and Helen felt the room cool slightly. A silence grew between them as they entered a sort of impromptu staring contest.

"I'm sorry," Helen said finally, her voice small and weak. "I'm sorry if I said something wrong or-or offensive."

"It's a highly... personal question among my kind. To reveal your exact nature - and especially to reveal your lineage - is to reveal your weaknesses."

Helen waited, unsure if she should speak.

"G1 to F3," Luciana said at last. "And I hope you will forgive me for not answering your question. I trust you, Helen, but I have survived centuries on this Earth for a reason."

Helen was flabbergasted, and it was no doubt written all over her face. Judging from the sudden smile on Luciana's face, Helen looked ridiculous.

"You look a bit surprised with your mouth open like that," Luciana hid her smile behind her hand.

"Did you say you're *centuries* old?"

"Yep," she nodded firmly.

"Is that, is that fairly old for your kind or?"

"It's hard to know, even for us," Luciana shrugged. "Once upon a time, there existed great cities of our kind. These days we tend to seclude ourselves, or else gather in small communities. For those of us on the outside, we don't exactly get much news. Though I will say, when one of the Ancients dies, it causes a stir that's quite impossible to miss."

"How impossible?"

"Have you ever heard of the Great Fire Of London? The blazing inferno that lasted four days and left the city decimated?"

"Jesus."

The pair fell into quiet introspection, their chess game unfolding at their feet, but the conversation otherwise fairly stifled. Almost an hour passed and there was still no clear winner, but there was a building sense of regret that Helen could feel pouring off Luciana.

"Are you... alright?"

"I'm a bit... remorseful?"

"Remorseful? Why?"

"I'm afraid I've scared you off."

"Scared me off? Are you kidding me?"

"Well, it's not exactly-"

"Luciana you're *amazing*! You're gorgeous and powerful and mysterious and my *god* do I find you-"

Luciana interrupted her, closing the distance between them in a few short steps, grabbing ahold of her face with a hand on each side, and planting her lips firmly against Helen's. Their kiss deepened, and Helen wrapped her arms around the taller woman's waist and pulled her close. At long last, however, she pulled away and looked closely at Luciana's face.

"So, can you tell me more, or should I change the subject?"

"As long as you know there are things I can't answer," Luciana shrugged, "then that's fine."

"You'll let me know if I cross a line?"

"I promise."

Helen chewed her bottom lip, desperately wanting to know more but also keenly aware that Luciana's boundaries were as-yet-undiscovered.

"Alright, erm-"

"Don't forget it's your move," Luciana nodded her head at the board. "Can't have you dodging this loss after all."

"Oh in your dreams," Helen laughed, turning her attention to the board again.

Helen was in a good position, though she had suffered heavy losses. Of her original sixteen pieces, she was down to five, not ideal given that Luciana still had eight.

"E5 to C3, check."

She watched the small icon of her queen slide soundlessly across the floor to its appointed spot, a studious frown on her face. The move was risky, but unless-

"E4 to D2."

Luciana's response was nearly instant, her knight sliding into a sacrificial position that - oh shit, how had Helen missed it? With the knight

170

moved, and her own queen pulled away, she'd left herself more vulnerable than she thought.

"I thought you said you were a casual fan," Helen grumbled good-naturedly.

"I find that definition to be true," Luciana grinned. "Besides, I *can't* lie."

"What do you mean, you can't lie?"

"It is physically impossible for Fae to lie, but anything shy of that is fair game."

"Holy shit," Helen thought back to the countless white lies she'd told over her lifetime. "Even small, innocuous things?"

"Not even that."

"Are there other restrictions you have?" Helen held her hand up and stayed Luciana's response. "Things you're comfortable telling me."

"Well, being unable to lie means we have to keep our promises," Luciana continued. "If a Fae promises to do something, they *have* to do it, period."

"So when you said that I could look at all that art as long as I liked?"

"I meant it, we can go right now if you want," Luciana smiled again. "So long as you concede the game, of course."

"Hmm, I don't think so-"

"G7 to G1," her grin broadened. "Check."

"Damnit," Helen sighed. "E1 to E2."

Three more moves and Helen was pinned, irredeemably doomed.

"Alright, fine," she couldn't help feeling a bit deflated. "I concede."

She held her hand out to shake with Luciana, but a commotion on the board took her attention. She'd been impressed enough when they moved on their own and even more so when the captured pieces had sunk seamlessly into the floor, but now the victorious black pieces were replaced with sparkling orbs of light that shot up about three feet and popped in soundless showers of glittering sparks. The miniature firework display lasted about twenty seconds and when the last shimmering embers faded into nothing, Helen noticed the board was completely reset - ready for the next game.

"Does it always do that?" Helen sighed good-naturedly. "Or are you just showing off?"

"It always does that," Luciana laughed and grabbed Helen by the waist. "But you *are* pretty enough to show off for."

"Oh flattery does *wonders* for me."

"Noted, noted."

Luciana let go and sat down in one of the plush armchairs nearby. With a small wave of her hand a wineglass - complete with dark red wine - appeared in her empty palm.

"You said you had more questions?"

"I do," Helen sat down in a chair next to her. "Starting with 'can I have one of those?'"

"Hold your hand out."

Helen did, extending her hand nervously and bracing herself for whatever might come. She watched as her host moved the fingers of her free hand in a swirling, unpredictable pattern. She saw the faintest hint of an orange glow at Luciana's fingertips. Helen was staring hard and was *just* on the edge of figuring out the pattern when a sudden weight filled her hand. The glass of wine didn't appear gradually, but it was somehow not so instant that she could grasp it right away. It was some combination of the two, and the smoothness of the transition from 'not there' to '*there*' left Helen speechless.

"Do you ever get used to it?" she brought the glass to her lips and took a sip, savoring the deep oaky flavor.

"To the wine?"

"No," she laughed. "To freakin' *magic*!"

"Honestly, no," Luciana shrugged with a smile. "But it's a part of me, part of my very being. To a Fae, magic is as vital as breathing, as liberating as standing on a seaside cliff, and as thrilling as a rollercoaster."

"God, I can only imagine," Helen took another sip of wine and leaned back in her chair.

"So, what else do you want to know?" Luciana locked eyes with her.

Luciana's eyes had the same hungry glint from the night before, a peek inside the *energetic* woman sitting across from her. The woman's robe was loosened, her hair still messily framing her face from their morning activities, and she was swirling the dark red liquid in her wine glass with tantalizing slowness, but it was - as ever - her piercing eyes that captivated Helen the most.

"Honestly, I don't even know what to ask, at this point," Helen breathed. "I still can't believe this is all real."

"It is though," Luciana gave her a reassuring smile.

Helen settled into a silence that grew less and less comfortable. She wanted desperately to be present, to simply enjoy this time and this space, but the nagging, ever-present voice in the back of her mind asked '*what if.*'

What if this isn't real, what if this is just you when you've gone fully off the rails? Maybe you're not even crazy, maybe you're in a coma in some Oklahoma ICU, and this is your brain's way of-

"Penny for your thoughts?"

Helen snapped out of it and smiled weakly at her host. Drawn suddenly back to the present, she shook her head and re-focused on her surroundings.

"Sorry, I-"

"You apologize a lot," Luciana took another sip of wine, a crease appearing in her forehead as she frowned. "Did you know that?"

"Yeah, sorry," Helen shrugged sheepishly and took a gulp of wine to steady her shaking hands. "It's uh, it's kind of automatic?"

"Hmm."

Helen waited, certain her host would say more. As the moment lengthened, however, she realized with dismay that Luciana must still be waiting for an answer to her question.

"I was worrying," Helen broke eye contact and looked down into the dark red liquid in her glass, studying the shimmery way the light played on its surface. "About... well about all this being..."

She trailed off into a mumble, still too anxious to meet Luciana's gaze again.

"It must be difficult for you."

Helen's ears perked up, and she risked a glance at Luciana's face. Her host had a somber, almost mournful look. Her eyes were stormy, and the crooked smile Helen had grown accustomed to, was now down-turned. Even the glow she had about her had dimmed and dulled.

"It's um," Helen wrinkled her brow in thought. "It's a challenge, b-but I try not to let it define me, you know?"

"That is wise," Luciana's voice was low but firm. "Because it doesn't. You are so much more than your…"

"Disorder."

"*Condition*."

Helen scoffed instinctively.

"You disagree?"

"I agree that you can be 'more than your condition' with things like blindness, deafness, chronic illness even-"

"But not with bipolar disorder?"

"You don't understand."

"Of course I don't," Luciana's reply was as unapologetic as it was instant. "I don't have to face this particular struggle."

"It's like I'm walking blindfolded across a narrow bridge," Helen sighed. "On one side, there are sharp rocks waiting to crush and impale me. On the other, there's a steep decline made of ice that would send me rocketing faster and faster out of control."

"That's a very… specific mental image," Luciana was smiling again, though she was clearly trying to contain it.

"Oh, and the bridge is made of unsupported glass," Helen hung her head, unwilling to let Luciana see her own smile as she considered the ridiculousness of her metaphor. "And like, has no freaking railings."

"Meaning at *some* point the bridge will crack, even if you stay on it?"

"Even if I walk straight down the middle," Helen nodded. "I could walk perfectly centered, but at some point the floor is going to fall out from under me and I'll be headed one way or the other."

"So then your medication would be…?"

"Supports under the bridge, and handrails on either side," Helen willed herself to relax, but she could feel her heartbeat throbbing in her neck and her chest tightening with every breath. "They keep me safe. Or *safer*, I guess."

Helen scrunched her eyes shut and worked on circular breathing, counting her way up 1-2-3 while breathing in, holding for 3, and then breathing out again 1-2-3.

"Sometimes, sometimes it gets hard for me to distinguish what's *real*," Helen admitted, her eyes still shut. "The more off course I get, the worse it becomes."

"That must be frightening."

"It's terrifying," Helen suppressed a shudder. "Questioning everything and everyone around myself is enough to send me spiraling all by itself…"

"I wish I could help somehow," Luciana's sadness was palpable. "That there was something I could-"

"Wait a minute," Helen popped her head back up, eyes open. "Wait a second, *couldn't* you help me?"

"Helen-"

"You could just magically make some of my medication appear, couldn't you?"

"Helen, that would be so dangerous," Luciana frowned. "I've never made modern medicine before. I have no idea if it would be formulated correctly, or the right-"

"But then couldn't you like," she snapped her fingers, "*fix* my brain?"

"Absolutely not," Luciana's sudden heat stopped Helen mid-syllable. "It is *deeply* forbidden to use magic to manipulate a sentient being's mind."

The temperature in the room rose noticeably, and Helen saw flecks of glowing orange swirl in Luciana's pupils. Her host seemed suddenly much larger, her figure imposing even from her seated position. Helen blanched and tried to stutter out a response, but failed. Luciana must have realized the terror clutching Helen's heart because she deflated just as quickly.

"I'm sorry, Helen," she shook her head. "But you must never, *ever* ask a fae to do something like that again - not even me. Do you understand?"

"I'm s-sorry," Helen mumbled, close to tears. "I didn't-"

"Helen, hey," Luciana stood and approached her, kneeling at Helen's side and clasping her trembling hands. "Hey, you couldn't have known. I'm sorry my reaction was so… visceral."

Luciana's hands were like the light of the sun, warm and soothing. Helen could feel the woman's touch pulling the tension out of her muscles, and for the first time in several minutes, she let her shoulders relax.

"I shouldn't have pressed you," Luciana kissed Helen delicately on the back of her free hand. "I'm truly sorry."

"Now who's scaring who off," Helen sniffled.

"It'll take a lot more than that to scare me," Luciana reached out and lifted Helen's chin until their eyes met. "I'm a big, terrifying, magical monster, remember?"

"You're not a monster," Helen snorted.

"Neither are *you*."

Helen's breath caught in her throat, and she squeezed Luciana's hand to hold back tears.

"Can... can we change the subject?"

"Of course, what should we-"

"Can you tell me what on earth is going on with this library?"

Luciana's face was a painting of surprise, and Helen giggled as she saw her host cycle through shock, confusion, and then, finally, understanding.

"What, you mean the books?"

"Yeah," Helen sniffled again. "Like, your books are backwards, upside down, every which way except the right way up!"

"Oh blah, who wants to do things the normal way anyhow?"

"So there's really no rhyme or reason?"

"I didn't say that," Luciana grinned, her eyes twinkling brightly.

"So then…"

"Many of these books have magical titles, things that can activate upon reading, regardless of the intentions of the reader," Luciana explained. "Some are so delicate, I cannot even show you - someone who can't read the inscriptions - without them triggering."

"Are they dangerous?"

"Some of them," she shrugged. "Others are simply 'jokes' among my kind, which are sometimes also dangerous but funnier, I suppose."

Helen looked around the room, at least half of the books were placed in some unusual manner, could they really all be magical?

"What sorts of magic uh… *stuff* would be in these?"

"All sorts of things, but many of them are histories, journals, biographies, and autobiographies."

"So no spell books and grimoires? That's disappointing."

"Disappointing?"

"Yeah, I just figured there would be like 'tomes of ancient knowledge and power' or whatever."

"Who says there aren't?"

Helen's face lit up like a candle in a dark room. Her mind was filled immediately with images of massive dusty leather bound books humming with power and filled with scrawling, glowing script.

"Can I *see* one?"

"It would be too dangerous, I'm sorry."

"Oh come on," Helen begged. "You've got some then?"

"I do."

"So that's what's on the third floor," Helen scratched her chin and took a sip of her all-but-forgotten wine.

Luciana laughed brightly and shook her head in obvious appreciation.

"You are extremely perceptive, you know that?"

"Yeah, well good luck convincing my mother of that," Helen shot back with an eye roll.

Luciana latched on to the subject change and quirked an eyebrow.

"That brings to light an interesting point," she stood and pulled Helen to her feet. "You haven't really told me much about your life."

"Ugh, what's to tell," Helen groaned, downing the last of the wine in her glass.

She moved to set the empty vessel down on a nearby end table, but it was refilling itself out of thin air until it was once again full of burgundy wine.

"That's a neat trick."

"I find it much more convenient than lugging a bottle around," Luciana winked conspiratorially. "You were saying?"

"Was I?" Helen asked as Luciana led her out of the room. "Where are we going?"

"You said you wanted to see the gallery again, did you not?"

Helen smiled brightly with delight, increasing her pace until she and Luciana were side by side.

"So you're from Tennessee?"

"Yeah, born and raised actually," Helen sipped again, realizing only now that she was a bit buzzed. "My mother and father and I lived in downtown Nashville until his music career started to take off."

"And then?"

"And then he... he was gone. It was just my mother and me," She shrugged. "Mom sort of lost it and took me out to the 'burbs."

"What does your mother do?"

"Other than criticizing my every waking moment?" Helen sighed deeply, her thoughts turning toward home. "She's a forensic accountant."

"*What* is a forensic accountant?"

"She goes over corporate and criminal financial records to determine potential wrongdoing," Helen pulled ahead of Luciana and began applying steady pressure on the woman, dragging her toward the gallery. "She's got her own firm and she's a consultant for the Nashville Police Department, the local FBI field office, and the Nashville and Davidson County Sheriff's Offices."

"Your kind invents the most absurd professions," Luciana smiled, slowing down even more. "Still, she sounds like a very capable woman."

"Capable of giving me a pounding headache maybe," Helen was sweating slightly from the effort of trying to move her host. "Jesus christ are all Fae this-"

"Strong?"

"*Stubborn.*"

Luciana burst out with laughter, her infectious smile bringing joy to Helen's face as well.

"I am a fair sight taller than you," Luciana planted her feet and Helen found herself completely unable to budge the larger woman. "Besides, I have a gym, remember?"

"Oh my god," Helen dropped Luciana's arm in surprise. "You *didn't* have a gym before, did you!"

"I did not, I had to... adjust the house so as not to lie to you."

It was Helen's turn to laugh out loud now, and she felt the remaining tension of their earlier discussion wash away as she appreciated the absurdity of magically creating an entire gym just to avoid an innocent white lie.

"That's amazing," Helen said, wiping a tear of mirth from her eye.

"I'm glad you approve," Luciana smiled back. "But to answer your question, no, not all Fae are physically strong. Those of us who are more... durable, are so because of the path we've chosen to reach our current form."

"So it's either a sign of your lineage or a sign of your age, Basically?"

"Or both," Luciana nodded down the hallway.

Helen, following her gaze, realized that they'd made it to the gallery at last. She squealed with delight and yanked open the door. Helen didn't even wait for Luciana to invite her in, she crossed the threshold in a heartbeat and was instantly enraptured once again.

Chapter Eight

"Helen," Luciana asked after a while.

"Hmm," she replied, not looking up from the statue she was studying.

"What did you study while you were at school?"

"Mathematics and Business," she stood up and eyed her host quizzically. "Why do you ask?"

"Is that... is that what you *wanted* to study?"

"It's a good area of focus," Helen frowned. "The coursework was intense, but it teaches marketable skills that-"

"That's not what I asked though," Luciana leaned back on the chaise lounge she'd summoned.

The furniture looked like it would be at home in some Sultan's opulent suite at the height of the Ottoman Empire. Plush cushioning covered in fine red silk and sturdy mahogany wood bedecked with glittering gold supported her host while she lounged like an oversized house cat.

"No, it wasn't," Helen answered at last, drinking in the sight of Luciana lounging and drinking wine. "I didn't want to have anything to do with either major."

"So why did you?"

"They made sense," Helen reiterated. "Plus I'm *good* at both."

"And?"

Helen's frown deepened as she stood once more.

"And they were my mother's idea, happy?"

Luciana's eyebrows rose, but rather than respond she took another deep drink of wine.

Helen took Luciana's silence as surrender, and returned to studying the marble sculpture in front of her. She tried to lose herself once more in the way the artist had so meticulously carved the lines and creases in the woman's palm, but Luciana's line of questioning had well and truly pulled her from her musing.

"I wanted to study history," Helen blurted out at last, risking a glance up at Luciana. "With a focus on art and antiquities."

Luciana's gleaming smile emboldened her to speak on, and she straightened up and moved to the next piece.

"My mother said it was a ridiculous choice, that appreciating art is a hobby at best and by no means the foundation for a career," her jaw tightened at the memory of all the times they'd fought around the dinner table. "She was right, of course."

"Was she?"

"You don't agree with her?"

"I don't," Luciana shrugged and looked off into the distance, unintentionally striking a pose that stole Helen's breath away. "I think that life without passion is not life at all."

"Passion doesn't pay the bills," Helen pointed out, pausing a moment to think before continuing on. "Speaking of which, what do Fae do for, like, work?"

"Work," Luciana laughed. "Why on earth would we 'work' at all?"

"Well how do you pay property taxes, your electrical bill, your... I don't know, your... whatever else you need?"

"Well, being old has its merits," Luciana smiled. "I have a great many things that I've simply collected over time that would be considered museum quality artifacts. I personally am an avid collector of coins, for example."

"You collect... coins?"

"Laugh if you want to, I have a stack of two dozen gold dollar coins from 1849 up in my bedroom in perfect uncirculated condition."

Luciana's proud, serious passion brought a wide smile to Helen's lips.

"Oh, I see," Helen replied with faux seriousness. "And how much has the value of your twenty four dollars grown?"

"Erm well," Luciana paused for a moment. "Math is more your strong suit, I'll wager, but around 650,000 dollars, give or take?"

Helen stumbled mid-step.

"Ok I was kidding at first but, you're like… *loaded.*"

"Material wealth isn't really something I ever *meant* to accumulate," Luciana said with a shrug, her tone apologetic. "But like many of my kind it sort of… comes with the territory."

"I guess I hadn't considered that," Helen gestured at the sculpture in front of her. "Not to mention all this artwork, it must be worth-"

"Oh, I could *never* sell my art!"

"But you *are* a collector, obviously."

"Well, in a way, I guess."

"You guess," Helen indicated the room with a sweeping gesture. "What do you call all of-"

She froze, her eyes narrowing, and looked back at the sculpture she'd just been studying. The white marble depicted a woman resting on a chaise lounge. The subject was reclining, one hand gently resting palm down, and the other holding a wine glass to her lips.

Helen glanced back and forth between the sculpture once, twice, three times to be sure before pointing an accusing finger at her host.

"Wait a second," her face turned red as her eyes widened. "*Your* art... This is you!"

Luciana's cheeks reddened and she appeared lost for words, which Helen took as a sure sign that she was correct.

"I thought you said you couldn't lie!"

"I *can't*," Luciana sputtered indignantly. "I never lied to you!"

"You said you didn't know who made these."

"No, I said that it was 'an excellent question,' and that 'Their work only exists here,'" she huffed, "Both of which are true!"

Helen's eyes narrowed.

"I'm beginning to understand the whole ' trickster fae' thing," she crossed her arms.

"I... I don't feel *comfortable* talking to people about my art," Luciana admitted. "I get embarrassed."

"How on earth could you be embarrassed by this?" Helen stepped closer to the woman. "These are amazing. Like, the museum-quality kind of amazing."

"Helen..."

"No, seriously," Helen spun around slowly. "You made *all* of these?"

"I did," she mumbled. "And about ten thousand more that are even worse."

"Will you do one of me?" she asked quietly.

"You want me to make a painting of you?"

Helen blushed, but nodded fervently.

Luciana hesitated.

"I've only very rarely painted someone other than myself," she scratched her chin absentmindedly. "I'm not so sure."

"Please," Helen begged. "I'll do anything!."

Luciana's crooked smile told Helen she might be winning the war, but the stubborness in her eyes said it wasn't over yet.

"Only if you'll help me."

"Help you?"

"Mhmm," Luciana nodded. "Come on, let's go to my studio."

Helen rushed over excitedly, and was practically glued to Luciana's side as they made their way from the gallery back to the library, then up the staircase to the second floor. Here, Helen paused, her gaze drawn upward to the mysterious, as-yet-unseen third floor.

"Now now," Luciana pulled her from her reverie. "No need to go up there, right?"

"Right," she jumped, hurrying down the hallway after her host. "No reason at all…"

The pair made their way towards the end of the hall opposite from where Helen's bedroom was, and stopped about midway through.

"You're sure you want to do this?"

"Absolutely," Helen beamed. "Why wouldn't I?"

"Alright," Luciana sighed, pushing open a broad wood door. "Come on in."

Helen gazed around with wonder as she entered the studio. It was unlike any other room she'd seen in the house so far. The walls lacked the wooden paneling she'd grown accustomed to, and instead were blank white plaster. Rather, they may have started out white, but now there were smears of color everywhere. Paint, pencil, oil, pastel, charcoal, and every other medium imaginable, had found its way haphazardly spread across the walls.

There were dozens of unfinished paintings in various stages of completion, some on easels and others leaning up against the walls. There were half-hewn blocks of marble, a pair of dirty pottery wheels, even a stack of plastic-bagged blocks of fresh clay tucked away in one corner, as well as a large wooden crate stuffed with what looked like torn paper and canvas. Racks and racks of paint brushes, jars, and dozens upon dozens of other art supplies - both recognizable and unrecognizable - filled every imaginable space.

"This is crazy," Helen said, awestruck. "It's like an art teacher's dream."

"Well, I certainly don't think I'm qualified to be a teacher," Luciana laughed. "But I like to explore different mediums and well, frankly when I get in a mood to create, I want to have things available, you know?"

"Well couldn't you just use magic to get what you need?"

"Oh no," Luciana shook her head. "I refuse to use magic for any part of my creative process."

"Not even to get materials?"

"Not even that," Luciana's tone left no room for argument. "I send Armand to get me supplies when needed, or I order them in from a catalog."

"Oh my god, you still use catalogs?"

"Yeah…"

"Right," Helen laughed, making her way towards the crate of discarded artwork. "When exactly is the last time you updated your technology around here?"

"Erm, I had the phones installed in 1935," Luciana cast her eyes skyward in concentration. "And I believe the wiring was updated in 19….88?"

Helen tried to formulate a response, but she found herself utterly unable to make words. She must've been a sight, as Luciana cracked a wry smile that she tried unsuccessfully to hide behind her hand.

"Shall we?"

Luciana nodded across the room, inviting Helen to walk with her, but Helen still wanted to investigate the bin next to them.

"What are these?" she said, finding her voice at last and reaching in to grab the nearest crumpled canvas.

"Don't!"

Luciana reached a hand out in desperation, causing Helen to freeze in place.

"Sorry. Please don't look at those, they're discarded for a reason."

"Could it be... Are you a perfectionist?" Helen teased gently.

"As old as I am, I have no excuse to be anything less than perfect," Luciana crossed her arms. "I hate making mistakes. Making mistakes gets people-"

Helen waited for Luciana to continue, but her host seemed deeply uncomfortable and unwilling to continue.

"I'm sorry, Luciana," she reached out and hugged the other woman tightly, laying her head against her chest. "I didn't mean to upset you."

"It's fine," she smiled weakly. "We all have our quirks, right?"

"Right," Helen tilted her head up. "So where do we-"

"Follow me."

Luciana led her to the far corner of the room where an easel was set up. A tall stool sat behind the easel, and a multi-tiered shelf with paints, brushes, and other implements. On the other side, in front of the easel, there were chairs, a small couch, and a variety of hangars with colored cloths to hang behind a subject.

"Go ahead," Luciana nodded, taking a seat. "Get comfortable."

"Erm…"

"You know," Luciana didn't look up. "Grab something to sit on, take a seat and just... pose how you'd like, alright?"

"Any way I'd like?"

Something in Helen's tone made Luciana's head snap up and she was graced with another of those wicked smiles that made her melt.

"Yes," she raised an eyebrow suggestively. "Unless you want me to help?"

"I would, actually," Helen felt heat returning to her chest and face. "If you could paint me any way you'd..."

Her voice trailed off as Luciana set down her materials and approached her. The woman's height pulled Helen's gaze upward and she found her breath catching in her throat.

"May I?"

Helen nodded, her mouth suddenly too dry to speak.

Luciana stepped past Helen, close enough for her to feel her body heat. Helen had to focus on her breathing to make sure it didn't stop. Luciana paused at a particular piece of furniture. The chair, a deep burgundy affair with a high, curved back and brass trimmings, settled in the center of the corner facing the easel. Helen turned to head for the chair, but then paused. She heard a soft gasp as, with a quick tug, she pulled loose the belt on her robe and let it fall off her shoulders to settle in a small heap at her feet.

"Is this alright?" she looked shyly over her shoulder to meet Luciana's devouring eyes.

"If you're comfortable," Luciana nodded, "then sure."

Luciana strode to the chair, crooking a finger to indicate that Helen should follow her.

"Have a seat," Luciana said. "Ok, now this leg over the other, and lean this way… perfect."

Helen bit her lip as Luciana settled herself behind the easel, suddenly feeling very exposed and wondering why on earth she'd decided to do this in the nude.

"Is there anything else you'd like in the painting with you, or a color palette you'd prefer?"

"Something um… warm, I guess?"

"Perfect," Luciana nodded as she selected a number of small jars of paint and a few brushes from the shelf beside her.

The woman snapped her fingers and in an instant the robe she was wearing was replaced by a paint-stained pair of canvas overalls. Her hair was up in a messy bun and held back by a dark blue bandana and her relaxed face had been replaced by a serious, focused expression.

"Oh," Helen exclaimed, drinking in the sight of her. "That looks very professional."

"It might interest you to know that I've painted this way since the 60's," Luciana smiled back. "1963, actually."

She sighed wistfully, lost in thought for a moment, before shaking her head and returning her attention to Helen.

"So, how were the sixties?" Helen asked as the woman finally began to set paint to canvas.

"The sixties were great," Luciana mumbled back. "Many Fae were able to travel more freely. It was a more... relaxed time."

"It's so odd," Helen studied her host. "I keep forgetting you're... um... well you're..."

"Old?"

"Shit," Helen buried her cherry-red face in her hands. "It was not supposed to sound like that!"

"I suppose I *am* old," Luciana smiled. "Though I believe I prefer the term 'experienced' if you don't mind?"

Helen was too embarrassed to reply, so she simply nodded firmly.

"I believe we were in the middle of painting you?"

Another nod.

"Then relax a little!"

Helen spent the next thirty minutes studying her host. The woman was intensely focused on her craft, carefully selecting each brush and jar of paint before meticulously applying it to a rectangular canvas set upon an old worn wooden easel.

The silence was warm and comfortable, as was the room. From Helen's vantage point sprawled across the over-sized chair, she could see at least a dozen half-finished projects. A ripped charcoal drawing sticking out of a trash can about ten feet away caught her attention. The drawing had been torn into several large pieces, but Helen could make out a stunningly beautiful face with ebony skin and tear-filled eyes.

"Who's that?"

"Hmm?"

Luciana didn't even look up, instead she squinted at her painting with a faint frown. She reached up absentmindedly to rub her forehead with the back of her hand - leaving a streak of dull orange paint behind - and returned her brush to the canvas.

"Luciana?"

"Huh, what?"

The intensity that her lover held as she looked up at last was contagious, and Helen felt herself swept along by the passion, the *drive* of the woman.

"Who's that?" she asked again, pointing to the discarded drawing.

"Oh, er, well that was a friend of mine... a long time ago."

"Why throw it away?"

"I can never get it right," she sighed. "And she deserves for it to be right."

An unexpected pang of jealousy crawled across Helen's mind, but she brushed it away.

"Was she... Fae?"

"She was, yes."

The sadness in Luciana's voice, paired with the far-off distant stare, told Helen not to pry but... she was desperately curious.

"Where is she now?"

"She died," Luciana wilted. "She died a long time ago and I feel very responsible for it."

"What *happen-*"

"Can we change the subject, please? I shouldn't have left that lying around."

"You're right, I'm sorry."

Helen started to stand, to move over to Luciana's side, but the woman held her hands up and tutted her until she retook her seat.

"Don't move *now*," she frowned sternly. "I can't have my muse moving all around before I'm finished!"

By the time Luciana finished her work, some thirty minutes later, the warm comfortable atmosphere had returned and Helen felt at ease once more. Luciana pushed back from the easel, streaks of paint on her face, neck, and arms, standing brightly against the cinnamon color of her skin.

"Done already?"

She nodded with surprising shyness.

"Can I see it?"

"Come on over," Luciana beckoned her with a flick of her head.

Helen stood, scooping up her robe and pulling it on as she worked her way around. Her jaw dropped as the painting came into sight. Most of the picture was blurred, soft warm yellows and reds blended seamlessly into sunset-like oranges. In the middle, much more defined, was a woman sprawled across a high-backed chair. She would swear the woman was her, but she'd never been that beautiful a day in her life. It captured every crease and line, every fold and plane of her body in exquisite detail, right down to the color of her eyes behind her glasses.

"Oh my god," she whispered, utterly at a loss for what to say.

"You like it, I hope?"

"Luciana, it's beautiful," she turned back to her still-seated host. "Much, *much*, more beautiful than I have ever-"

Luciana stood, planting a kiss on Helen's lips that cut her off mid-word. As the kiss lengthened, it deepened as well, and soon Luciana's arms were curling around Helen's shoulders even as Helen's were gripping tight to Luciana's waist.

"You're getting paint all over me," Helen giggled when they came up for air.

"Is that so?" Luciana teased back. "We wouldn't want that, would we."

Helen opened her mouth to reply but found herself blinking in shock as a wet paintbrush drew a thick line down her cheek. She stared at the offending item - floating in the air courtesy of Luciana's magic - but her shock turned to laughter as a large glob of red paint dripped off of it and onto Luciana's bare shoulder.

"No, of course not," Helen pushed away, grabbing a brush from beside the easel at random and flicking paint at Luciana, who laughed as she tried to duck the aquamarine splatter.

Within minutes the pair were splattered with every color of the rainbow, and tangled in each other's arms atop a once-white sheet on the ground and breathing hard. Helen was a good wrestler, or so she figured, but Luciana was bigger - and stronger - and was presently pinning her down to the floor. Luciana had a wrist in each hand and sat astride Helen with a pressure that was beginning to warm more than just her face.

"Do you yield?" Luciana whispered in her ear before nibbling gently at her neck.

"And what if I do?" Helen challenged her, seeking her lips out. "What then?"

"To the victor go the spoils, right?"

Helen's giggle of agreement turned to a moan as Luciana found a spot on her collarbone that made her eyes roll.

"Jesus, Luciana," she whispered breathlessly as the woman pulled her hands over her head.

"Hmm," Luciana nibbled Helen's ear as she transferred both of her wrists to one strong hand, and ran the other lightly up her pinned lover's side. "Are you a christian?"

"Right now, I'm whatever you want me to be."

"As far as answers go," Luciana pulled back a moment, visibly drinking in the sight of Helen's paint-splattered body. "That was *very* sexy- oh!"

Helen used her host's distraction to plant her feet and buck up, rolling over and ending up atop Luciana. The woman's shock lasted long enough for Helen to pin her arms at her sides, held there tightly by Helen's thighs while she sat just above her stomach but below her breasts.

Helen reached a hand out to stroke Luciana's face, absentmindedly smearing a streak of brilliant yellow across her warm skin. The woman's pulse was visible in her neck, thinly covered by a blob of fine cerulean, and her collarbone - one of the few places left untouched by their escapades - drew Helen's eye to the rapid rise and fall of her full breasts beneath the worn overalls.

In their tussle, one of the two clasps holding the garment on had come undone, and all but the nipple of Luciana's left breast was laid bare.

"God you're beautiful."

"You know I could lift you easily," Luciana smirked, her eyes glinting brightly.

"Oh?" Helen laughed, tightening her grip. "I've got pretty strong thighs, I wouldn't be so sure."

"Such confidence," Luciana smiled wider, her hands curling up and her long slender fingers tracing lazy circles on the backs of Helen's thighs and just below her backside.

Helen leaned in close, a hand on either side of Luciana's face, and kissed her deeply. Their tongues danced, exploring each other as Helen's core turned molten.

"*Prove it.*"

Helen yelped as Luciana's arms lifted her as easily as a bouquet of flowers. She gasped and fell forward, barely catching herself with her hands as Luciana gripped her rear firmly and pulled down on her hips. Helen's gasp of pain from the stinging in the wrists, turned to a breathless moan of pleasure as Luciana buried her face between Helen's thighs.

The silky softness of Luciana's cheeks and lips contrasted deliciously with the warm, wet, textured strokes of her skilled tongue as it danced between her labia. Helen's fingers dug into the dropcloth below them and her hips began moving of their own accord, grinding against Luciana's hungry mouth. Luciana, rather than pull back, drew Helen closer still. She clamped down on the tender skin of her backside, her nails digging into Helen's skin and her palms locking her in place.

Luciana's tongue dove deeper and deeper, twirling, flicking, and rolling in ways that felt impossible to Helen. Soon she was hunched over, her breath ragged and her thighs trembling as she raced toward a climax as bright as the sun. Helen felt her vision spin as Luciana - as though she could sense Helen's impending orgasm - pressed on with renewed vigor. Luciana dragged her tongue roughly along the length of Helen's vulva, her tongue ending its journey at her clitoris where it circled with a firm, steady pressure.

Helen's trembling turned to a wild shaking and she cried out as her nerves burst into flames, lightning made of pure bliss rocking through her body and reducing her to a quivering mess. Luciana pressed on until Helen saw stars and it took all of her strength to croak out a single word.

"O-o-okay," she gulped for air. "Okay... ohmygod, I... s-slow down."

Luciana's hands relaxed instantly and Helen felt her head pull back.

Looking down, Helen took stock of Luciana's slick, smiling face. She was breathing hard - beads of sweat dotted the woman's brow and her cheeks, chin, and lips were soaked with Helen's essence.

Helen crawled unsteadily backward as Luciana rose to a sitting position, bringing them face-to-face.

"Well," the woman's dark, glittering eyes teased her. "Did you enj-"

Helen reached out one hand, taking a fistful of Luciana's jet-black hair, and brought their lips together. She could taste herself on the other woman's lips, and it further stoked the flames inside of her.

"How fast can you get out of those overalls?"

Chapter Nine

Helen had long since lost track of time, but as she lay tangled with her lover in a pile of drop-cloths and fabric scraps, she couldn't care less. They were both naked, Luciana's overalls were tossed thoughtlessly on the floor a few feet away, and Helen was resting her head in Luciana's lap while the woman sketched absentmindedly in a small notebook.

Helen's eyes were closed, but she could tell by the faint scratching and rubbing of the pencil across rough, high-weight paper that her host was lost in her art.

"What're you drawing?" she mumbled, nestling her head more comfortably on Luciana's thigh.

"Tr-ng to sketh you."

Luciana's garbled words caused Helen to crack one lid and look up at her. Luciana had two different pencils between her teeth, and a stick of charcoal behind one ear.

"You know you could just set those down right?"

"I'm uthing them," Luciana glared in a way that was impossible to take seriously.

"Mhmm, alright," Helen yawned widely. "You're the pro, not me."

Luciana cast Helen an apologetic glance and set her pencils down.

"I'm sorry," she raked a hand through her tangled hair. "It's late and you're tired."

"Is it?"

"Is it what?"

"Late," Helen sat up, one arm holding a paint-splattered cloth across her chest. "How late?"

"The sun's already set," Luciana frowned. "A little after seven o'clock?"

"How can you tell the sun's down?" Helen searched one-handedly through their nest for her clothes.

"The same way I can tell the moon started rising over two hours ago," Luciana shrugged. "All Fae can feel the ebb and flow of the sun and moon."

"That," Helen's comeback was punctuated by another yawn. "is a pretty neat trick."

"Are you hungry?"

"I'd rather get cleaned up first, honestly."

"Right," Luciana stood, gently removing herself from the cloth surrounding them and scooping up her overalls as she headed for the door. "This way to the shower."

"Shower?"

Luciana paused, turning back in surprise.

"Would you rather have a bath or?"

"N-no," Helen found her clothes at last. "I'm just surprised you don't use magic to get clean."

"Oh gods no," Luciana shook her head. "And deny myself the genuine pleasure of a hot, steaming shower?"

"I suppose that's fair," Helen moved to follow her.

"Besides," Luciana led the way back into the hallway and turned toward the library. "You know heated showers have only been around for a couple hundred years? You try living with nothing but a washbasin and tell me how much you appreciate a good shower!"

Luciana continued to lead and Helen was more than happy to admire her as she moved gracefully through the manor. The woman's stride was utterly shameless. She looked comfortable in her own nudity in a way that Helen envied, and even the scars marking her back were perfectly suited to her copper skin.

"Where did you get those?" she finally worked up the courage to ask.

"Get what?" Luciana paused, her foot hovering over the floor in mid-step.

"Those scars," Helen suddenly felt as though she was prying *too much* and felt red color her face.

"Ah," Luciana continued down the hallway, albeit a little more stiffly. "I used to be in a dangerous line of work."

"So you… retired?"

"You could say that."

"Is that why you're here, at Casa De Rosas?"

"Yes," Luciana turned towards her bedroom suite. "I suppose I got tired of the... costs associated with it."

"Do you want to-"

"Change the subject?" Luciana looked back with a sad smile. "Yes, please."

"Right," Helen smiled back, kicking herself internally as she felt the heat of the evening cool a bit.

Do you seriously not know how to stop prying? Jesus.

"The shower is through here," Luciana held open one of the many doors in the suite, revealing a large room of slate gray tile and dark bronze accents.

The word shower was an understatement. One entire corner of the bathroom was sunken down about four inches from the rest of the flooring. In the center of the space was a large drain in the shape of a rose blossom, and hanging from the ceiling was an elaborate network of thin bronze piping that looked for all the world like a cluster of rose vines.

The corner of the space held a low tiled bench, which had a few expensive looking bottles of soaps and shampoos. The walls here were a mosaic of blues and greens, and a pair of brass knobs inset into the glass looked to control the water.

"That's a shower?"

"You get old enough and you start to enjoy the finer things," Luciana laughed, dropping her clothes in a pile and stepping down into the shower. "Come on in."

Helen dropped her clothes on top of Luciana's and stepped down as well, curious where exactly the shower head was. She didn't have to wonder long, however, because Luciana promptly stepped over to the knobs and gave them a spin.

Helen gasped as the bronze above let loose a gentle shower of perfectly warmed water. Every thorn on the vines above was apparently a small nozzle, and the effect was a soft, steady rainfall of steaming comfort.

"Oh *god*," Helen closed her eyes in ecstasy. "I could get used to this."

"I'd love to help you with that."

Helen looked at her host in surprise, and could swear she saw a hint of red in the woman's cheeks before Luciana turned away and grabbed one of the bottles from the bench.

"You like lavender?"

"Mhmm, of course I do."

Luciana sprinkled a few drops from the bottle around the shower and soon the air was filled with the sweet, relaxing perfume of fresh lavender.

"You weren't kidding about the finer things."

"Well, I told you I couldn't lie, didn't I?"

With the size of the rainfall shower above them, there was more than enough room for both of the women to clean up without feeling cramped, and without either of them being stuck out in the cold at all. Luciana's collection of toiletries were beyond fancy, each in its own glass or crystal bottle and bearing Italian or French writing on their elaborate labels. Helen was in no rush, and it seemed that Luciana was just as content to dwell in the warmth as she was.

Helen was sure that most of an hour must've passed by the time Luciana finally turned and asked if she was ready to towel off. Helen's muscles begged her to stay, but her pruney fingers told her that perhaps it was time to get out after all.

A few minutes later they were both wrapped snugly in thick fluffy bathrobes and headed back to the bedroom of the master suite. Helen was surprised to see a platter of meats, cheeses, and fruit not unlike the others she'd had during her stay.

"You eat a lot of this stuff," she remarked, popping a grape into her mouth.

"I'm not much of a fan of so-called modern cooking," Luciana shrugged, selecting a rolled up slice of prosciutto and a piece of gouda. "I don't like to eat heavily early in the morning or late at night - I think it makes more sense to eat simply and cleanly."

"No wonder you're ripped," Helen sighed, eyeing Luciana with appreciation. "I don't eat clean by any stretch of the imagination."

"Ripped?"

"Uh, well-muscled," Helen explained. "I forget that you're not up to speed on slang. How long have you been cooped up here?"

"I'm not *cooped up*," Luciana frowned. "I… well, alright, perhaps I am a bit cooped up."

"A while then?"

"I got out for a little while in the forties, then again in the sixties," Luciana's expression clouded over. "But things… didn't work out. Some things never change, that's all."

"It sounds unbearable," Helen suppressed a shudder. "Being alone with myself is the *last* place I ever want to be."

Luciana reached out and took Helen's hands.

"It sounds like maybe you've got some healing to do then."

"Ugh," Helen looked away briefly, then shot Luciana a frustrated smile. "You sound like my therapist!"

"I'm sorry, I don't mean to lecture," Luciana laughed. "Please, sit. Eat."

Helen obliged and sat down on the side of the bed, patting the comforter and smiling when Luciana sat down beside her. The pair shared a comfortable silence as they worked their way through the hor d'oeuvres.

"Wine?"

"Mhmm? Oh, sure!"

Luciana summoned a sauvignon blanc and a pair of glasses, the wine lightly chilled and superbly crisp. The bottle emptied while the stars beyond the bedroom windows slowly spun through the night.

They finished their first bottle, and were well into their second before Helen knew it. She had a delightfully strong buzz, and felt very warm and relaxed in the presence of the beautiful woman beside her. Her mind was just foggy enough to be quiet, and her tongue was loose and honest - in between her sizable yawns.

"You're too good to be true," she announced with only the slightest slur.

"I'm not, but I appreciate the sentiment, Helen-"

Helen interrupted her with a kiss, moving her free hand to Luciana's thigh.

"Easy, Helen," Luciana smiled, pulling back after a moment. "You've had quite a bit to drink and you're-"

"I'm fine," Helen giggled. "I'm in college, I know how to drink."

"This isn't mortal wine," Luciana put a hand to Helen's cheek and rubbed it gently with her thumb. "Another side effect of magic is that it slowly inundates everything around it. Many things become more... potent. Especially alcohol."

Even as she spoke Helen could feel her buzz escalating to true drunkenness. Rather than slow her down, her few remaining inhibitions began to fail and the fire inside of her burned hotter and brighter.

"Luciana, I think I'd like to kiss you again," Helen set her glass down. "I'd like to do a lot more than-"

"Helen, darling, I can't allow it. You're gorgeous and I'd love nothing more than to repeat our earlier exploits with you, but you're definitely drunk and in no condition to agree to anything quite so... intimate."

Helen sighed heavily. Even in her current state, she couldn't find a good argument with Luciana's words. That said, her host's chivalry was doing nothing to quench the heat she felt.

"You're right, you're right," she raised her hands in surrender. "I should go to bed, right? Yeah, I should go to bed."

Helen moved to stand, and suddenly realized just how intoxicated she truly was. No sooner had she made it to her feet than the room began to spin violently.

"Oh shit, wow."

"Helen? Where are you going?"

"I'm ok," Helen closed her eyes and took a deep, slow breath. "I'll be alright once I make it to my room."

"Oh."

Luciana's voice was unmistakably sad, and Helen looked over at her with surprise.

"Wha's wrong?"

"I-it's nothing, I just had rather hoped you might want to sleep in here tonight? With me?"

Helen woke to a feeling she had missed the last few days - warm clear sunlight on her skin. For a moment, she was disoriented, but the feeling quickly passed. She stretched widely, feeling the satisfying crackle of her joints as she shifted around to look over beside herself.

Luciana was still asleep, and for the first time since they'd met, she was not perfectly composed and flawless. Her hair was a mess, her mouth slightly open, and the tiniest line of drool was pooling on the fine silk of her pillowcase. The woman's breaths were slow and even, but her brow was furrowed deeply as though in concentration.

Helen couldn't help but wonder what she might be dreaming about. What *would* an immortal dream about? The past, or perhaps the future? With so many memories, would they need to dream at all or would they simply think back on their past experiences?

Helen made a mental note to ask Luciana when she woke up, but for now she was content simply to lay beside the woman and drink in her beauty. Her skin, which had appeared bronze in the low lighting of the cloudy skies of the past few days, now was closer to burnished copper. Her skin was smooth and unblemished, and the light sheets covering them hugged her sleeping form like an angel in a renaissance painting. She watched as Luciana's face scrunched up, and felt the woman's leg twitch under the covers and had to stifle a chuckle, but quiet as she was, it looked like her host was already on her way to waking.

"Good morning," she whispered as Luciana's eyes fluttered open. "You're adorable when you sleep, you know that?"

"Ugh, Gods, I forget how easily humans lie," Luciana groaned, wiping drool from her chin with a corner of the bedsheet before running her hand through her tangled curls. "I'm a mess and we both know it."

"No, really," Helen objected, laughing. "You don't look so... so perfect. It's nice."

"Mhmm, I guess I have no choice but to believe you. Breakfast?"

"Sure, but I have two questions."

"Go for it."

Luciana sat up, the blankets covering her falling to her waist and looked down at Helen. For her part, Helen was too flustered to speak right away. She felt her cheeks redden and she tore her eyes away from Luciana's figure and looked her in the eye once more.

"*That* was distracting."

"I could say the same thing," Luciana nodded at her, and Helen realized that her own torso was fairly exposed, as was one of her legs all the way up to the hip.

"Fair enough."

"So, your questions?"

"First, what's for breakfast?"

Helen's stomach chose that moment to gurgle loudly, eliciting laughter from both of the women.

"Whatever you'd like, we can probably accommodate pretty much any request."

"Damn, that's pretty nice," Helen considered the ramifications for her waistline if she had access to any food she wanted, whenever she wanted it. "So like, if I said bacon, biscuits and gravy, and over-medium eggs, you could just snap your fingers and make it happen?"

"Well, technically, I guess you could reduce it to that. What really happens is the refrigerator fills with whatever I want it to, and then Armand cooks it for me."

"The *fridge* knows what you want for groceries," Helen's jaw dropped in disbelief. "And who *is* Armand anyway?"

"That's a third question," Luciana pointed out. "He's my butler, my porter, my confidant, and I suppose for many years, he's been my only real friend."

"That's a non-answer, is he also a Fae?"

"No, he's not Fae."

"So he's human then?"

"You're starting to get the hang of this 'no lying' thing," Luciana sighed. "No, he's not human either. He's a construct, a sort of magical object imbued with a semblance of life."

"Have you always had him around?"

"No, he joined me in the late 1800's when it became less popular to be an unmarried woman. I created him to... keep up appearances."

"Ok, ok, second question-"

"Sixth question, technically."

Helen frowned, then stuck her tongue out at Luciana.

"Ok *sixth* question then. Are all Fae sticklers for technicality?"

"Yes, we are. We are obsessed with rules, loopholes, technicalities, and the like. Many of our kind become lawyers just for the challenge of it, actually."

"I just *knew* there had to be a drawback," Helen sighed with mock seriousness.

"Very funny, so what is your second slash seventh question, since I assume that wasn't it?"

"You assume correctly. I was going to ask what the plan today is, since the weather's finally broken?"

"Well," a wide mischievous grin spread out across Luciana's face as she scooted closer to Helen. "There's the matter of our bet?"

"I believe the wager was-"

"A treasured memory," she smiled, a gleam in her eye. "But just to borrow, I promise."

"I'm not sure how you can *borrow* a memory," Helen felt a sudden nervousness. "Actually, wh-what *does* that mean, exactly?"

"Fae crave experiences, emotions," Luciana explained, tucking an errant strand of Helen's hair behind her ear. "We have the ability to… well, I guess to *consume* the memories of others - if they are given willingly."

"Hang on," the hairs on Helen's neck prickled. "You're going to eat my memories?"

"Only temporarily," Luciana reassured her. "Though I could simply consume them, Fae also have the power to give them back."

"I thought I was just going to *tell* you about a memory!"

"Helen, I didn't mean to deceive you," Luciana's smile faltered.

"Why does it sound like there's a 'but' that you aren't saying?"

"A bargain struck is powerful magic," Luciana's expression fell. "It stems from the oldest days of Fae history and is more powerful than any of us."

Helen felt suddenly unsure. She was having trouble distinguishing between anger, frustration, embarrassment, and fear, and rather than lash out, she took a moment to turn inward.

"Helen, I'm sorry. If I could lift the magic I would, I would in a heartbeat."

"I'm sorry, Luciana, can, can you give me just a moment?"

Luciana fell silent and Heather concentrated on her circular breathing. She refused to let this be the straw that would break her back. She would master her emotions with or without her medication, and she would move forward.

"So what if I *don't* give you one of my memories?"

"Then there are magical penalties," Luciana looked down at her hands. "Generally, it does not go well. Usually 'misfortune befalls you until the debt is satisfied.'"

"So, that's why you're always saying 'there is no debt,' I take it? You don't want me to technically owe you anything for your hospitality?"

"Yes, I want you to know my warmth toward you is genuine, and that I am not taking advantage of you."

"What if I had insisted that I owed you?"

"Wording is paramount to Fae," Luciana explained. "To owe a Fae is a very dangerous position to be in, especially if no price was negotiated. Technically, an unspecified favor owed to a Fae could be redeemed for anything from a pretty rock to your firstborn child-"

"Ok, I have one," Helen interrupted, her brow furrowed and her lips set in a straight line. "What do I do?"

Luciana turned until she was sitting cross-legged with Helen directly in front of her, and gestured for Helen to do the same.

"This isn't going to hurt or anything," she promised. "But you'll relive the memory with me, then it'll sort of... fade. After that, giving it back is a much more instantaneous process."

"I'll just suddenly re-remember it?"

"Yep."

"Alright, here goes."

Luciana reached out and gently grabbed Helen's hands. The woman's skin was warm and soft and supple and the way she held Helen's hands reminded her of everywhere those fingers had traveled.

"Do you have your memory in mind? Be careful not to give me more than I'm owed."

Helen refocused, then nodded.

Helen's eyes snapped open, taking in the sights of the park around her. From her vantage point on a wide, plastic-seated swing, she could see all the way to the parking lot on her left and to the lake on her right. Wind rushed past as she reached the highest point of her swing, and her small hands gripped tightly to the old rusted chains of the swing as she began her backwards descent.

"That's it Helen," her father cheered. "You can go higher!"

The man's ruddy complexion and jet black hair tugged at her child-sized heart, and she was surprised to find that his scruffy five o'clock shadow, deep brown eyes, and wide genuine smile brought tears to her eyes. Helen picked up speed on her backswing, cupping her legs as she passed the midpoint and rocketed backwards.

She pumped her little legs, pink sneakers untied and laces flying in the wind, and pushed forward once again. The world rocked below her as she pushed herself higher and higher with every swing.

"Rich!"

Helen's mother, a picnic basket in hand, was headed over from the parking lot and she watched as her father turned toward her and waved.

"Rich, she's going to flip over the bar, are you nuts?" the woman laughed as she approached.

Helen's mother set down the picnic basket and shared a long happy embrace with her husband at the base of the swingset, then joined in cheering on their daughter.

"You can do it, baby!"

Helen felt herself continuing to build up speed and a thought entered her mind, a belief really. Perhaps if she focused hard enough she really could fly?

In the space of three more swings, she was convinced and her mind was made up. A scowl of determination crossed her small face and she pushed with greater purpose.

"Momma, papa," she shouted down to them. "I can fly!"

"Baby, you can't fly, ok," Helen's mom cast a concerned look at her dad. "Just swing ok? You have to stay in the seat."

"No, really momma, I can! I can fly, I know I can!"

"H-honey, honey listen to your mom, ok?"

"Yeah, baby why don't you just slow down a bit and we can take a break for lunch, alright? I brought sandwiches."

Helen was too focused, too determined, and she couldn't wait to see the expressions on their faces when she took off into the sky. A voice in her mind prompted her to push, *push* just a little harder. She came back for a final backswing, the scowl on her face turning to an elated smile as she rocketed forward and - just as she was reaching the zenith of her arc - launched herself out into the air.

Her mother's scream was drowned out by the rushing wind and the glorious experience of flying untethered through the air. She shut her eyes and soared, picturing what their faces must look like.

A resounding crunch accompanied by instant shooting pain marked her return to the earth as her shoulder impacted the hard grassy ground. She tumbled head over heels several times, battering her body all over before landing on her back with a wheeze. She couldn't breathe, all of her wind having been knocked out by the impact, and searing pain was radiating out from her shoulder and her knee.

Helen tried to scream, but couldn't catch her breath. She could feel herself panicking even as the faces of her parents - ashen with fear - swam into sight through the rivers of tears streaming down her face. Her heart felt like it was going to explode, and she could feel her pulse pounding in her ears.

"Helen, Helen!"

Helen gulped air as she snapped out of the memory. Her heart was still pounding, and beads of sweat dotted her forehead. Luciana had a hold of her shoulders and had clearly been shaking her.

"Helen, are you ok?"

"I-I think so," she tried to steady her breathing. "What happened?"

"What's the last thing you remember?"

"I was going to give," she paused to take a breath, "to give you a memory. I was going to give you the memory of… of… uh I don't remember."

"Ok, so you don't remember the memory at all?"

"No," Helen focused in on Luciana's eyes. "Why? Did something happen? Did something go wrong?"

"No, nothing went wrong, the magic worked," Luciana spoke in a low soothing voice. "It's just that normally the person giving up their memory doesn't feel things quite so intensely, and their memory fades much more smoothly and rapidly…"

"So there's something wrong with me?"

"No," she shook her head. "I don't think so. I think maybe you simply *feel* very deeply."

"So do… do I get my memory back now?"

"Yes, and it should be much less intense. Lean forward."

Helen leaned forward and felt Luciana place a palm on either side of her head. She felt a pop in her ears like she was in an airplane and jerked upwards, regarding Luciana with surprise.

"Holy shit, that was a trip."

"Your memory is...?"

"Yeah," Helen nodded, rubbing her temples. "Yeah it's back."

Chapter Ten

"Are you ok?"

Luciana's voice, normally so strong and confident, was soft and timid. The two women were sipping coffee in a solarium overlooking the grounds of the manor, and hadn't spoken in several minutes. Helen was lost in introspection and Luciana appeared too nervous to speak.

"Hmm?"

"Are you alright?" she repeated. "I'm so sorry, I didn't mean to-"

"That was the last time I saw my dad," Helen mumbled, her eyes welling up with tears.

Get ahold of yourself.

"Oh gods," Luciana's hand went to her mouth and her shoulders drooped.

"He was in a wreck that afternoon. My parents had driven separately because dad was just getting off work, and we were right behind his truck on the way to the hospital when... when..."

Helen felt herself drawing back from reality. She could feel herself detaching like a ship from its moorings, headed out to sea and safe from the dangers of land. She knew now that a word existed for this experience, 'dissociation' her doctors called it. She'd wavered between struggling against the sensation and embracing it, and over the years of her life, it had served her very well. It'd become harder to embrace since she started her medication, but it never fully went away. Sometimes she fought the feeling, sometimes she really struggled to maintain contact with her feelings, with reality.

But not today, not now.

Helen allowed herself to withdraw until she could practically see over her own shoulder. Until she felt as though she was simply watching a particularly personal TV show, or perhaps playing a third-person video game.

"It's alright," she gave a wan smile, trying to overshadow the flatness of her voice. "It was a long time ago."

"Right," Luciana sighed. "Would calling your mom help, or someone else maybe?"

A flicker of feeling reached out toward Helen's mind at the mention of her mother, but she swatted it away like a bothersome insect.

"Helen? Hey, come back to me," Luciana snapped her fingers, drawing Helen's attention. "You're scaring me a little."

"I'm sorry," Helen said as a pang of guilt stabbed her in the gut. "It's ok, I'm ok."

"You seem like you're kind of... not here."

"I don't like the way this topic makes me feel, so I'm choosing not to feel at all."

"You're choosing not to feel at all," Luciana repeated in disbelief. "Why would anyone choose to not *feel*? Even pain is better than nothingness."

"I think I'll make that phone call," Helen said abruptly, acutely aware of the distress on Luciana's face but unable to make herself deal with it emotionally. "Is that alright?"

"Of course."

Helen scooted back, the legs of her chair grating against the tile flooring. She rose and turned to the archway that led to the rest of the house. By now she had a firm grasp of the layout, and it only took her a few minutes to walk across the manor to the office she'd called from a few days before.

All was as she'd left it, even the cushy, formal looking leather chair that was offset from its normal place behind the desk. The phone was still sitting just as it had been, and it was no less menacing than it had been before. Helen set aside her doubts, picked up the receiver, and dialed in the digits to her mother's house.

"Hello?"

"Hey mom."

A silence grew between them for several painstaking seconds before her mother spoke again at last.

"That's it? 'Hey mom' is all you have to say?"

"Sorry."

"Precision, Helen, precision. What are you sorry for?"

"I'm sorry I hung up on you so abruptly before," Helen grit her teeth, anger threatening to penetrate the shield of numbness protecting her heart. "And for not having a better greeting for you."

"*Right, are you safe?*"

"Yes, mom, I'm safe."

"*Where in Oklahoma are you, I'll come pick you up.*"

"I'm honestly not exactly sure," Helen ran a hand through her hair nervously. "I got washed off the road in the storm and landed in a river. Well, it could've been a creek or a stream at some point but it was-"

"*Washed off of what road? Into what body of water?*"

"I was trying to figure that out when I got knocked into the water, mom," Helen began pacing. "I made it east of Oklahoma City but I missed the highway somewhere."

"*So where are you, what 'friend' are you staying with?*"

Helen ground her teeth at the unmistakable sound of air quotes in her mother's tone.

"My car took out a small bridge, and I got pulled out by a gal that lives-"

"*A woman pulled you out of a wrecked car in the middle of a flooded river? Oh please Helen-*"

"Yes, mom, a woman pulled me out of a wrecked car in a flooded river," she snapped back. "Am I telling the story or not?"

"*Temper, Helen, temper.*"

"She pulled me out and took me in, I've been staying with her until the storm dies and they can get someone out to fix the bridge enough for me to cross."

"*Well, can't she just give you a lift? Take a different route?*"

"It's a private bridge to her property, there is no other way out-"

"*Oh, well that's pretty convenient.*"

"Not for me it isn't!"

"*Isn't it though?*" Helen could hear the condescension dripping from her mother's words. "*You're the one who chose to drop out, you're the one who wanted to come home. I take my time to make everything-"*

"Mom! Jesus christ, this wasn't a *decision* I made," Helen shouted. "I didn't drive off the road for kicks!"

"That's not funny, Helen," her mother's words were ice cold. "Don't joke about that, you know how I feel about you making those jokes."

Helen hung her head, different trains of thought all criss-crossing through her mind.

"Are you taking your medication?"

"I… Yeah, I'm taking my meds."

"Helen, don't lie to me," her mother scolded. *"You know what happened last time you went off your meds."*

"Yeah, I know mom," Helen glanced down at the long straight scars - now pale and faded - that ran halfway from her wrists to her elbows. "I know. I'm safe, I promise."

"Helen-"

"Mom, I didn't call you to fight with you dammit. I just… I just wanted to talk to you, not get a lecture. Please."

"*I worry about you, Helen, I won't apologize for that.*"

"I'm not asking you to," Helen took a deep, steadying breath. "Mom, what *happened* to us?"

"*What do you mean-*"

"After that day in the park, when I broke my shoulder and dad… after dad's accident."

Helen could sense her body's distress, like listening to a car alarm from under water. She could feel her heart rate climbing and a tightness growing in her chest, and her throat began to close until she felt like she couldn't swallow and could barely breathe. The world outside her protective bubble threatened to break in, to break through the curtain of numbness she'd wrapped herself with, but she was too well practiced and her defenses were too strong.

"*You know what happened Helen, or are you having an episode?*"

"I'm not having an episode I-"

"*Your father died. He was in a car wreck right in front of me while we were driving you to the hospital, is that what you want to hear?*"

"Us."

"*What?*"

"Right in front of *us*, mom."

"*Is that what this is about? A pity party-*"

"I meant when did you get so *cold*," Helen punched the wooden desktop in front of her with her free hand. "When did you-"

"*Don't you dare speak to me like that, Helen Marie! I am your mother,*" her mother was screaming now, something Helen hadn't heard in many years. "*I lost my best friend that day, so don't you dare tell me I'm cold like I didn't have a reason, like I didn't lose my whole world!*"

"Your *whole world*," Helen repeated softly. "Nevermind, mom."

"*Helen wait, don't hang up-*"

Helen set the receiver down with a soft click and found herself standing awkwardly in the silence of the room. A tickle on her hand drew her attention and she looked down. She was surprised to find that three of her knuckles were bleeding, and she watched with detached interest as blood ran down her half-curled fingers and dripped on the floor.

A soft tapping at the door made Helen turn. She was moving slowly, her mind dedicated to cutting the invisible threads of emotion that still tied her to the phone on the desk. She could picture it clearly, a shining pair of scissors floating in the air snipping through bright red cords tying the antique phone to Helen's heart.

Snip. Snip. Snip.

"Yes?"

Helen's voice was low, soft, and distracted, but the door swung open nonetheless.

"Madam," Armand gave a bow. "My lady Luciana would like to speak with you, at your leisure."

"She wants to speak with me, am I in trouble?"

Another string to cut?

"Not at all ma'am, she sent me to ensure you were well."

"I, ok. Where is she?"

"She's in the library, madam. Will that be all?"

"Yes - no, actually can you bring whiskey sours to the library for us? Is that like, a thing you can do or?"

"Do you have a preference for whiskey, madam?"

"Anything, just don't put a cherry in there, please."

"Very well, madam," Armand bowed once more and backed away, shutting the door softly as he went.

In a better headspace, Helen might have paused a moment to address the issue of her knuckles. In her present state, however, the injury was already out of her mind.

Her feet were nearly silent as she worked her way back toward the library, her mind and expression equally blank and her footsteps wandering and purposeless. It might've taken her ten minutes, or it might've taken her an hour - she truly didn't know. Helen was surprised to see Luciana pacing one wall of the library, rather than seated. She paused in the doorway, absorbing the scene in front of her.

Armand was standing as still as a statue beside a pair of high-backed chairs, a silver tray with a pair of rocks glasses on in it one of his white-gloved hands. Luciana was chewing her nails as she wore a track in the tile below her feet. Helen must've made a sound as she approached, because Luciana looked up suddenly and froze in her tracks.

"Helen," she chewed her lip. "I'm so sorry, I shouldn't have pressed you like that and-"

A pang of guilt slipped through Helen's defenses.

"It's ok, I'm fine. Sorry to worry you, Luciana."

"Did you talk to your mother?"

"Are those the whiskey sours?" she crossed the room, already knowing the answer, and grabbed one of the glasses.

"I'll take that as a yes," Luciana mumbled, meeting her in the middle and picking up the second glass. "How did it go?"

"I'm not overly upset about being unable to return home at the moment."

"Right," Luciana looked down at her feet. "How worried do I need to be Helen, honestly?"

"Do you trust me to answer honestly?"

Should she?

Luciana took several long moments before she answered, and at first Helen thought she might simply avoid the question entirely.

"I do. I do trust you to give it to me straight."

"I'm... choosing not to feel strongly about it."

"Meaning?"

"Meaning I've decided to let myself dissociate," Helen lifted her chin defiantly. "I don't really care what my shrink says, I don't have the energy to deal with this right now."

She braced herself for another argument, certain that Luciana's response would echo her therapist, or worse, her mother.

"Alright, I understand."

"Wh-what?"

"I understand," Luciana shrugged. "This is your brain's way of protecting itself, and I would imagine it's kept you-"

"Alive?"

"I was going to say safe, but yes, alive," she stepped closer to Helen. "And alive is how I prefer you, if you don't mind?"

Luciana's response was... unexpected. It shook Helen firmly enough that she allowed cracks to form in her barriers, and guilt, sadness, and hurt came flooding through.

"Can I make it up to you?"

"There's no debt," Helen smiled thinly.

"Hey, that's my line," Luciana teased gently. "Please, I insist, I want to help you feel better. What can I do?"

Luciana took a sip of her drink, then reached out with her spare hand to brush Helen's cheek.

"Fine, show me the third floor."

Luciana's mouth popped open and her eyes widened with surprise. Helen took no small amount of joy in the flabbergasted expression of her host and couldn't help breaking out in a true, genuine smile.

"Helen…"

"Nope, that's what I want. I've decided."

"Alright, follow me."

It was Helen's turn to be too shocked to respond right away.

"Really?"

"Yes, really," she smiled, turning around and stepping away.

Helen gulped down the rest of her drink and set her glass down on the tray Armand was holding.

The glass clattered against the metal, causing Helen to flinch instinctively.

"S-sorry, Armand, sorry."

Armand didn't reply, which by now was unsurprising. Helen turned back toward Luciana and hurried to catch up. To her surprise, her host walked past the staircase and headed towards the foyer instead.

"Are we not going up?"

"We are," Luciana replied cryptically. "But we have a stop to make first."

Helen felt her heart sink a little. Was Luciana not going to take her up after all? Was this a consolation prize instead?

She's lying to you, this is a trick.

She shushed the voice in her head, causing Luciana to pause and turn.

"What was that?"

"Sorry," Helen blushed. "I was just talking to myself."

"Alright," Luciana smiled warmly.

Luciana headed to the front door and insisted on holding it open for Helen before walking through herself. As Helen stepped out into the world, she felt all the rays of the sun shining down on her, wrapping every inch of her in warmth and light.

She took a few steps forward and closed her eyes, tilting her face to the sun with her arms at her sides. There was a soft breeze, just enough to rustle her hair and tease her clothes; it was cool and refreshing and full of that unique freshness that fills the air at the end of a storm. Helen took a deep breath and felt the revitalizing power of the outside world being pulled in through her nostrils and filling her from within.

Helen had always had a deep connection to the outdoors. It contrasted oddly with her disorders, but in nature she had always found a certain comfort and the sense of connection that she craved. Something about this place - magic no doubt - magnified the effect.

"Coming?"

Helen opened her eyes, surprised that her host was standing about fifteen feet away.

"Coming where?"

"Did you think this was it," Luciana laughed softly.

"To be honest," Helen shuffled her feet. "You wouldn't be the first person to think they could cure my depression by making me go outside to 'get a little fresh air.'"

"Helen," Luciana stepped toward her, her eyes suddenly sad. "Oh Helen, I know it doesn't work that way. I'm sorry that people don't understand. I'm sorry that *I* don't understand, but I will not insult what you're going through by trivializing it.

Luciana held her hand out toward Helen, who stepped forward and grasped it firmly. She hoped the woman couldn't feel her trembling as she tried to contain the sudden rush of emotion she felt. If Luciana *could* tell, she gave no indication. Instead, she simply turned back to the grounds and, with a gentle tug, led Helen out onto the still wet grass.

"So where are we going then?"

"It isn't far."

Luciana led them across patches of grass, between vine-covered columns, past crumbling statuary, and between the boles of mighty trees before she came, at last, to a stop.

"Where-"

Helen's jaw dropped as Luciana stepped out of the way, revealing a massive, ornate structure made of glass and wrought iron. It was a green house, a massive one, that had to have been fifteen feet high and at least as big as a basketball court. The walls were entirely constructed of a patchwork of reclaimed windows, very, very old ones by the looks of them. Most of the windows were different sizes, creating a patchwork effect that dazzled the eye. Some of the glass was frosted, some clear, and there were even a few areas of a vibrant stained glass. Between the panes was black wrought iron with a dark patina, and there was a large french door inset into the side of the structure that was constructed in the same way.

"This is one of my other hobbies," Luciana announced proudly. "This - is my greenhouse."

"Luciana, this is stunning. You built this?"

"I did," Luciana beamed in a way that brought a smile to Helen's lips as well. "Back when I first came here. It is one of my favorite places in the whole world."

"Can we go in?"

"It would be fairly cruel to bring you here and then deny you," she winked. "Go ahead, explore."

Helen practically ran to the doors. She pulled them open swiftly but gently, and stepped inside.

The greenhouse was humid, and the air was thick with different scents. She recognized some of the plants - the sizable herb garden for example - but the vast majority of what she saw was as foreign as it was wondrous.

She wandered past benches and tables of plants, pausing every now and again to ask a question of Luciana, who trailed just behind her.

"Wait a second," she stopped in front of a small, peculiar looking bush. "That's crazy, that looks like a tiny pineapple on top there. What is that?"

"That *is* a pineapple."

"Bullshit," Helen's eyes widened. "Pineapples grow on *bushes*? They don't grow on trees?"

"I cannot tell a lie, remember?"

Helen burst out laughing, the absurdity of learning a new and random botanical fact in *this* environment of all places hitting her unexpectedly. She laughed until her sides hurt, until she was practically wheezing.

Keep it together, not like this.

She tried to stop herself, to force herself to shut her mouth and to swallow the laughter, but she was less and less in control of it by the second. She laughed past when she thought it was funny - long past. After about ten seconds, her eyes were welling up with tears and her laughs were sounding more and more like sobs, and it was all she could do to turn away from Luciana in shame.

"Please don't look at me right now," she managed between her hysterics. "Please."

She stepped away, trying to hold the flood gates closed until she was out of earshot - or at least out of sight. Her feet dragged her away and she desperately hoped that Luciana wasn't still watching. She ducked around a row of tall plants, then past another, and came upon a small reflecting pool with bright gold koi in it.

When Luciana finally found her, she was sitting on the dirt floor, arms wrapped around her legs, and face buried in her knees.

Helen heard her approach and tried to stifle the last of her tears, but her shoulders were still shaking when Luciana's hand landed on her back.

"Helen?"

"I'm ok," Helen mumbled. "I'm so sorry about that."

"Helen, there's nothing to apologize for," Luciana sat down next to her. "Can you help me understand? Or at least tell me how I can help?"

"I hate laughing," Helen pretended she was speaking to her knees so she didn't lose her nerve. "Especially when I'm upset. I hate it because laughter makes me feel... out of control. Like I am literally not in control of my body."

She lifted her head and stole a glance at Luciana, who looked puzzled but attentive.

"I don't know why it happens, but when I laugh really hard, it's like all the other emotions I'm suppressing just... bubble up. They burst out and it turns into a flood, a faucet I can't turn off."

"That sounds terrifying, Helen."

Helen let out the breath she was holding, surprised and relieved that Luciana understood.

"It is. It's like... it's like it grabs ahold of me and I have to fight like hell to try to get it back under control," Helen's volume rose. "People don't understand, they think it's *funny* when I beg them to stop making jokes or making me laugh. They think it's a game or something, and they-"

"Hey, hey," Luciana rubbed her back soothingly. "It's alright, I'm here ok?"

Helen buried her head in her knees once again, afraid that if she looked at Luciana's face, she would lose her grip once again.

"Let's try something, ok?"

"Try what?" Helen mumbled into her knees.

"C'mon, chin up," she felt Luciana rise beside her. "Follow me."

Helen peeked out and saw that Luciana was standing beside her, one hand extended to help her to her feet. Helen reluctantly accepted, and allowed herself to rise up. She stood there awkwardly shuffling her feet until Luciana gave a nod and headed deeper into the greenhouse.

"You know," her voice carried easily, even facing away from Helen. "In some ways, we aren't so different."

Helen snorted.

"Really. For example, this green house - all these plants - they're my way of trying to… connect."

"What do you mean?"

"Well, immortality is a strange blessing," Luciana's shoulders drooped. "Sometimes I catch myself wondering if a life without end is even a life at all, or whether I'm just *existing*. These plants, all of this life, it all makes me feel more *purposeful*. They tie me to the living, to life."

Helen pondered the woman's words. She'd never considered that immortality might be a burden. Then again-

Why ponder immortality when you never planned on living this long at all? You'll give in eventually.

She shuddered, ignoring the goosebumps that sprang up all along her arms.

"Here we are," Luciana announced, dropping Helen's hand, and turning around to face her. "I hope you don't mind getting your hands dirty?"

Helen wrapped her arms around herself and looked around. This part of the greenhouse was filled more with tools and empty pots than with plants.

"I don't get it."

"Let's plant something," Luciana smiled brightly. "Give it a shot at least, please?"

"I don't really know what I'm doing."

"Fair enough. Grab a pot from over there," Luciana pointed to a stack of clay pots. "And I'll grab some soil, ok?"

In short order, they had assembled all the supplies needed and were now standing side by side at a wooden workbench.

"Most every plant needs the same things," Luciana took a small metal trowel and scooped rich, dark earth from a burlap sack into a pot. "Everyone knows what they are - earth, water, and light, right?"

"Right…"

"But it's so much *more* than that," Luciana pulled open a drawer to reveal a dozen or so large, plump acorns. "If you look *beyond* the surface, what do those things mean? What do they represent? And what more is there?"

Helen was enthralled by Luciana's passion, but absolutely mystified as to what the woman was talking about. She watched as Luciana's strong fingers carved an indentation in the dirt and gently placed the acorn inside before softly piling a small mound of dirt on top of it.

"The dirt, with all of its minerals and nutrients, is a microcosm of the earth. It is strong, and forms the basis on which life can grow."

Luciana lifted her dirt-covered hands above the pot and rubbed them together. Helen gasped as water began to sprinkle down from between her palms - a tiny rainstorm just for this one seed to enjoy.

"Rain. Water. It pours down from the sky, yes, but it also flows through the earth," Luciana continued. "It runs beneath us, beside us, above us. Every drop of water has undergone the entire cycle of the world, endlessly since the beginning."

Next, Luciana raised her hands to the ceiling, tilting her face up and closing her eyes as a beam of sunlight hit the glass above. She was illuminated like an angel, drenched in radiance that grew to envelop the entire greenhouse. Helen could feel the temperature rise around her, but was surprised to find that it wasn't as oppressive as she would have expected.

"The sunlight," she took a deep breath and let it out slowly. "It warms us, it guides us, and it is the bright burning fuel that sustains us. At its core, it is *fire* that keeps us alive and enables us to survive and to thrive."

Helen's mind was now fully occupied with the woman beside her. This strange, impossible being held her attention like nothing else ever had. She watched as Luciana bent down low over the pot and drew in another long breath. The woman released the air in her lungs, softly blowing over the dirt. Helen felt the air stir around her, swirling around the workbench and out into the greenhouse, where it rustled leaves all around them.

"There's another thing these plants need," Luciana whispered. "The air, the *wind*. It carries carbon dioxide and oxygen and delivers their bounty to our lungs."

Helen watched as the dirt in Luciana's pot began to stir until a tiny flash of green appeared. At first Helen couldn't believe her eyes, but there was no mistaking that a pair of tiny green leaves were pressing their way into the sunlight. In the space of thirty seconds, the tiny plant grew into a foot-tall sapling.

"Luciana…"

She turned to face Helen, her cheeks flushed, and her eyes bright and excited.

"Earth, air, water, fire," Luciana's voice was rich and husky. "The elements of magic, the elements of *life*. Can you feel it? Can you feel the power in this place?"

Chapter Eleven

"I'm just saying," Helen laughed, her arms covered in soap suds up to her elbows. "You could run one hell of a flower shop, if you ever had the mind to."

Luciana rolled her eyes, taking her turn to rinse her arms and hands in the deep utility sink they were both standing in front of.

"Something about using magic to further grow my wealth through *flower sales* seems a bit..."

"Underwhelming?"

"I was going to say needlessly convoluted," she smiled. "I could go with a more classic maneuver - tricking silly humans into hopeless bargains in exchange for their riches."

Helen slid her hands under the cool running water as Luciana stepped back and picked up a towel.

"Speaking of bargains..."

"Ah, right," Luciana nodded, handing over the soft, terry cloth towel. "You are owed a certain something, aren't you?"

"Yes ma'am, I am!"

"Ugh," Luciana groaned. "Don't call me ma'am, I feel old enough."

Helen sidled up to Luciana and gripped her waist, running one hand up her back and the other down her hip and they locked eyes.

"You mean don't call you ma'am unless we're-"

"Yes," Luciana interrupted, her cheeks scarlet. "Yes, unless we're doing that."

Luciana tilted her head down and planted a kiss on Helen's lips, but quickly pulled back.

"But don't get me riled up or we might never make it to the third floor!"

Suitably chastised, Helen took Luciana's hand and allowed herself to be led back to the manor. It seemed that every time she looked at the towering, sprawling structure she noticed some new detail or accent. Those stone gargoyles perched randomly around the edges of the roof, for example.

Then again, there was every chance that they *hadn't* been there before, she supposed.

"Are the roses part of your hobby?" she asked, looking around at all of the blooming bushes around the property. "Or are those something else?"

"Um, a little bit of both," Luciana said, not turning to meet Helen's gaze. "But it wouldn't really be Casa De Rosas without the roses, right?"

"I suppose you're right," Helen shrugged.

She allowed Luciana to hold the door open for her - noting that for once, Armand was nowhere in sight - and headed back toward the center of the house.

"Listen, Helen," Luciana paused and turned to look at her guest. "You have to promise me a few things before I take you up, alright?"

"You're making me nervous," Helen joked, but Luciana's face remained serious.

"Ok, what am I promising you?"

"You can't touch *anything* unless I specifically tell you it's ok."

"Alright, I can do that."

"You can't go anywhere - and I mean walking, standing, crawling, jumping, anything like that without me telling you it's ok, alright?"

"Are we going to be in a minefield? What's with all the precautions?"

"My workshop is a place where active magic is taking place," she stared directly into Helen's eyes. "Some of the enchantments are dangerous if you interact with them. Dangerous and unpredictable."

A chill ran down Helen's spine, but she nodded confirmation. Luciana waited a moment more, then turned back around. The trip to the library seemed to take forever, and every second Helen's mind was conjuring up new and terrible outcomes for her visit to the third floor. Trepidation wrestled with excitement, and by the time they reached the smooth, cool tile of the library she wasn't sure if she even *wanted* to go upstairs.

Until she saw the staircase.

She could feel the power from before, drawing her heart upwards and pulling her toward the granite steps. Her nervousness was forgotten instantly, replaced by a growing desire to find the source of the pull. Helen felt the tug from up above intensify as soon as her foot landed on the first stair, and by the time she made the second floor, it took all her self control not to go sprinting past Luciana - who was suddenly walking with maddening slowness.

The stone stairs darkened as they moved up closer to the third floor, and the shadows around them deepened as well. There were several of the recessed lights that illuminated the rest of the staircase, but they were faint and felt somehow distant.

"These stairs seem longer than-"

Luciana stopped abruptly in front of her, cutting Helen's sentence short.

"Here we are," Luciana said, stepping up and disappearing out of sight.

Helen blinked, sure that she must have missed something. The stairs in front of her continued just as they had, but there was no sign of her host. She looked backwards, expecting to see the second floor below her. Instead, there was only a dark continuation of the stairs she was on.

You've lost it. You're finally gone. Just close your eyes and accept it.

Helen took a slow, steadying breath, and moved forward until she was standing on the last stair Luciana had been on. *Nothing* about her surroundings changed, but she refused to accept that this wasn't somehow real. Helen lifted her foot and took a tentative step forward.

A sudden, lurching feeling made her stomach roll, and she stumbled forward onto a stone floor that suddenly appeared below her foot in place of the step.

"What in the hell…?"

Helen looked around, Luciana was standing in front of her in the middle of a large room filled with a mind boggling array of strange and wondrous things.

"Helen," Luciana waved broadly. "Welcome to my workshop."

The energy in the air was palpable, and Helen could feel it as deeply as bass at a rock concert. Strange symbols, written in what looked to be charcoal, were scrawled on the floor, the walls - which were rough cut stone - and even the wooden eaves of the ceiling.

Fully half of the place was a library, though these books were mostly much thicker and older looking than the ones downstairs. Some of them were bound with ropes or chains, while others seemed, for lack of a better term, normal. She couldn't make out any titles, but before she tried too hard, she reminded herself of Luciana's warnings and looked away.

One whole section of the room was dedicated to different objects in glass cases, arranged in a manner that likely only made sense to Luciana. Another area was completely clear except for a massive charcoal drawing - though from this angle, it was hard to tell exactly what it was.

In another corner, racks and racks of bottles, dried plants, and other items were set against the walls, and a large cast iron cauldron was steaming away in front of them. Whatever was *in* the cauldron was a mystery as well, but judging from the swirling pink and green steam it was some manner of... potion?

Your girlfriend really is a witch.

"She's not my girlfriend."

"What's that?"

"Sorry," Helen blushed, hard. "Just talking to myself. What is all of this stuff?"

"Well," Luciana said. "This is where I create and maintain the magic that makes Casa de Rosas possible. It's where I have to do my daily rituals and where I... well, I guess humans would call it 'worship.'"

"Can you show me?"

"Follow me - closely."

Luciana led the way, heading to the cauldron first. It was deep, and about two feet across at the lip. The massive black iron object was partially inset into the stone floor, and there was a row of small hooks along one side of it. These hooks held tongs, a ladle, and a long spoon - all made from the same dark iron. Inside the cauldron was a bubbling, roiling liquid of the deepest purple. Every bubble that popped on the surface left swirls of metallic green and shining silver.

"This is a warding potion," Luciana picked up the spoon and gave it a slow stir. "It helps to generate the protective field around the estate, and to sustain the other protective measures."

"A warding potion. And this… this protects the whole property?"

"Among other things, yes."

"Where did you learn this stuff? Do all Fae just *know* magic?"

"No, we don't just know it," she laughed softly. "Or at least, we don't know most of it. We're all born with some innate knowledge though."

Helen took a moment to look around at the racks. Dried plants, a pile of rodent skulls, glass beakers filled with bones, vials of unknown liquids, even a palm sized rock that was levitating silently above the shelf.

"And all this stuff, where did it come from?"

"Most of it came from my life before this place," Luciana looked down at the floor. "The rest came from friends who took great risks to deliver things to me."

"Is that... not something that happens anymore?"

"No," she sighed. "Not for quite a long time. But it's better this way."

Helen reached out and grabbed Luciana's hand.

"I'm glad I'm here."

"I'm glad you are too," she smiled with genuine warmth. "Come on, let's keep looking around."

Helen could feel a deep vibration, so low and steady that at first she struggled to identify why it felt familiar. Suddenly it hit her, she'd lived a few blocks away from a set of train tracks as a kid, and even when she couldn't hear the trains, she could always *feel* them - like a localized earthquake.

She'd thought the feeling would subside once she reached the workshop, but if anything the pulling in her chest had only grown stronger. She found herself glancing more and more at the broad open space filled with charcoal markings - and couldn't tear her eyes away from the spot as Luciana led her past toward the books.

"These books are the ones too dangerous to take downstairs," Luciana gestured. "I have obscured their titles, so you should be safe to look at them, if you want- Helen? You seem... distracted?"

"I can't help it," Helen mumbled back. "There's something... calling me over there. Can't you feel it?"

"I'm not so sure we should go over there," Luciana's face took on an apologetic look. "It's the magical center of the workshop, the heart, if you will."

"I'm not sure I have a choice," Helen shook her head, not taking her eyes off the area to respond to Luciana. "I think I-"

"Alright, come on," Luciana tightened her grip on Helen's hand and led the way across the room.

As they approached, the design finally became clear. There was a massive pentagram, easily ten feet across. Each of the five arms of the pentacle were packed with writing - though Helen didn't know the language, or even the letters - and the entire ring around the outside was similarly inscribed.

There were five smaller circles equally spaced around the pentacle, each only about two feet in diameter, that had larger and more easily discernible symbols.

"Earth, water, air, fire." Helen muttered to no one in particular.

"That's right," Luciana was smiling brightly.

Luciana was emanating a sort of *hunger* that both unnerved and intrigued Helen, and something about this place - the power in the air - was stirring something inside of her.

"This is where I engage in my most sacred practices, and work my most powerful magic."

"It feels like," Helen took a sudden step past Luciana and into the pentacle.

Immediately she felt a wave of energy pass through her, electrifying her body and intensifying each of her senses.

"Helen!"

She stepped closer in, her feet moving without clear direction from her mind, and approached the center of the pentacle. Luciana, still holding tight to her hand, followed her in.

"Helen," she yanked on Helen's hand and spun her around.

Helen gasped as she found herself suddenly mere inches from Luciana and looking upward into her eyes. Luciana's hair was flowing softly, her eyes were glittering with light and her pupils were enlarged. Her skin was flawless, her lips plump and-

"Helen, this is a dangerous place for you to be," Luciana was clearly wrestling with herself. "This circle will magnify my feelings the same as it magnifies my magic."

"Is it magnifying my feelings as well?"

"Almost certainly," Luciana's voice was husky and low.

Luciana's hands found resting places on Helen's hips, and Helen felt herself being pulled closer until their bodies met. She could feel her breaths growing shallow, and the temperature in the room rose as well.

"Helen, I-"

Helen stepped up on her tiptoes and silenced Luciana with a kiss. A jolt of electricity shocked both of them as their lips met, and Helen let out a moan as a pulse of pleasure rocked through her body.

"Oh my god, what was that?" she asked, breaking away from her hungry lover.

"Sex, love, and passion are all powerful amplifiers of magic," Luciana slid a hand up Helen's side.

Helen suppressed another shiver as Luciana's hand came to rest below her chin. The woman's strong fingers gripped her gently but firmly, forcing her to make direct eye contact.

"That's *part* of why this is a dangerous game we're playing."

Helen bit her lip, unable to vocalize the fire ignited within her by Luciana's simple gesture.

"*Magnified* sounds pretty good to me" she whispered. "Maybe I'm feeling dangerous?"

Luciana groaned, but didn't let go.

"Dammit woman."

Helen didn't get a chance to respond, it was Luciana's turn to surprise her with a deep kiss. Their lips locked, but this wasn't the tender kisses of the past few days - this was rough and strong, and it made Helen melt.

Helen let out a yelp as Luciana bent down at the knees, grabbed hold of Helen's rear, and lifted her as easily as one might lift a gallon of milk.

"God you're strong," Helen managed between kisses, her hands reaching up and pulling her top off.

"And you're gorgeous," Luciana responded, lifting her higher and kissing a trail down her neck and onto her chest.

Everywhere the woman's lips landed felt like magma. Desire burned within her and pleasure radiated through her body like shockwaves. Helen's nails dug into Luciana's back, eliciting a shiver from her host.

"Where are you taking me?" Helen pulled back, her eyes focused solely on Luciana's. "Because I'm going to need you to - whoa!"

Helen held on tight as Luciana dropped to her knees, then leaned gently forward to lay Helen on the ground. She glanced over at the floor, surprised to find that they were in the exact center of the pentacle. She fit nearly perfectly in the pentagon around herself, and she could feel a heat from the wooden floor through her garments.

"Need me to what?" Luciana growled, leaning in low and nibbling on Helen's neck.

"I need *you*," Helen gasped between ragged breaths. "Fuck me."

Luciana sat up, leaving Helen feeling a cool breeze from her movement. She lifted her shirt up over her head to reveal a conservative black bra with a lace trim. She tossed her shirt to the side, with her bra following suit moments later.

Helen drank in the sight of her, until she met her gaze. Luciana's eyes were dark, intensely focused, and bored a hole deep into her soul. It was equal parts chilling and exhilarating. She looked like a hungry tigress about to pounce, and Helen was undoubtedly her prey. A trick of the lighting in the room - provided by flickering sconces evenly placed around the perimeter - made it look for a moment as though large, black, curved horns had sprouted from her temples and that a pair of wide black bat-like wings were spread out behind her shoulders. She blinked in surprise and the image was gone, leaving the devastatingly attractive woman in front of her.

"Open," Luciana said, her voice just shy of a command as she pulled Helen's legs apart.

Helen's breath caught in her chest. Luciana's push sent her skirt riding up her thighs to expose her distinct lack of underwear. She was grateful her cheeks were already flushed from desire, because Luciana wouldn't have been able to miss her blushing.

"Even better," Luciana murmured. "To what do I owe this pleasure?"

Luciana reached down with both hands, starting with Helen's knees and gently running her fingers down the inside of her thighs.

"All you have is lingerie and I didn't want to, I don't know, take advantage of your hospitality!"

Luciana's laughter was as soft and warm as her smile was wide and full.

"I told you," she scooted closer until she was between Helen's legs, their thighs buzzing with electricity where they met. "You are welcome to *anything* in this house."

"I really only want one-"

Luciana's fingers gliding across her soaking lips caused her sentence to sputter out like a candle in high winds.

"I've got a present for you then," Luciana grinned, holding her hands up.

The woman's fingers began to glow with a swirling green energy, capturing Helen's gaze and refusing to let it go. She slid her hands down her sides to her waist where she paused, her fingers swirling in more of the elaborate patterns she'd seen before. Everywhere her hands traveled dark black smoke followed. Luciana's left hand slowly worked its way around to her backside, while her right moved to between her thighs. Her head tilted back and her eyes glowed a brilliant green. She let out a moan of pleasure and a crackle of energy temporarily blinded Helen

When she finally blinked the light away, her eyes opened wide in surprise.

Luciana's body was decorated with a black lace bodysuit that hugged her body from her nipples to her hips, where it transitioned into more of a harness for-

Holy shit.

Between Luciana's legs was a crystalline strap-on, and a good sized one at that. The object was around seven inches long, and thick as any of her more adventurous toys. It was sleek, with a variety of ridges and swirls, and it had a gentle upward curve that promised to hit *just* the right spots.

"Where did-"

"You *did* say you wanted me to fuck you, didn't you?"

Helen hesitated, but Luciana didn't. She slid forward, grabbing Helen's wrists as she moved, and quickly had her pinned against the floor.

The strap-on was laying gently against Helen's entrance, the solid coolness of it contrasting starkly against the soft warmth of her core.

"Well?"

Luciana was leaning in close, nibbling on Helen's ear as she held her in place and expertly maneuvered the tool between her legs so that it brushed up and down the length of Helen's slit.

"I, what," Helen's mind was shutting down, all she could think about was the prize between her legs.

"Do you?" Luciana breathed, the head of her toy gently parting the very outside of Helen's lips. "Do you want me to fuck you?"

"Yes plea-oh my god," Helen's voice rose as the toy slid past her entrance.

Luciana pressed her hips forward, further spreading Helen's legs and filling her entirely as Helen rocked towards her, her hips tilting to allow her lover to bury the toy as deeply as possible. Helen's arms reached up to grab Luciana's strong, muscular back, and her feet planted themselves on the wood of the floor, toes already curling with pleasure.

Her clitoris was ablaze with sensation that was a match for any vibrator she'd ever used, despite the fact that it wasn't getting any direct stimulation.

"How are you doing that?" she panted.

"You'll find I'm full of surprises," Luciana purred, pulling out a few inches before rocking back forward. "Comfy?"

Helen nodded, biting her lip as Luciana thrust again, this time pulling further back and pushing forward with greater force. Her third thrust finally caused a whimper of pleasure to slip past Helen's lips, and her wicked grin was a sight to behold.

This can't be real.

Do we care?

Luciana's force and tempo increased steadily, her thrusts rocking through Helen's entire body and pushing her hips down against the floor below them. Helen was practically vibrating with arousal, and she could feel how easily the toy slid past her smooth, wet walls.

Helen pulled her hands free of Luciana's back, sliding her right hand across her stomach and then up to her breast, which she gripped firmly, her fully aroused nipple pinched gently between her clenched fingers. Her dominant left hand mirrored this gesture, but instead of sliding up her chest she snaked it down lower. She spread her first two fingers out along the inside of her labia, feeling Luciana's toy slipping in and out between them. She shivered with pleasure as she touched herself, her fingers sliding up and down her slick lips and circling her clit gently.

"Allow me?"

Helen, who hadn't realized her eyes were even closed, opened her eyes to look up at Luciana. The woman's hair was disheveled, her eyes bright, and her cheeks red, but she had yet to even break a sweat.

"Be my guest."

Helen's jaw popped open as she felt the toy inside her begin to pulse and vibrate, then felt her eyes roll back as invisible fingers began to mimic the motions of her fingers. Unseen hands gripped both of her breasts, and invisible fingers toyed with her nipples. She felt another of the invisible hands holding her face tenderly, while yet another brushed the hair gently from her face. The star of the invisible show, however, was the flurry of attention her clitoris and labia were suddenly receiving.

It felt like the work of four extremely skilled hands, even though when she finally glanced down there was in fact nothing there. Soft, tender fingers stroked around her clit, occasionally brushing across it. Others gently played with her lips, and still others danced along her thighs.

"Holy shit," her whole body trembled at the overload of sensations.

"Not yet," Luciana growled.

The woman's words were accompanied by a new set of hands, these firmly gripping Helen's ass and pulling her into every thrust, as well as a change in tempo from the pulsing toy between her legs. While the bulk of the toy was still pulsing together, a portion of the top changed its speed and grew more intense. This newly activated spot rubbed hard against Helen's g-spot with every thrust, and within a few minutes Helen was on the verge of sensory overload.

Helen bit her lip, forcing down the impending orgasm that threatened to rock through her entire body.

"P-please, Lu-ci-an-a" she moaned, every syllable interrupted by her lover's powerful hips driving the toy home. "D-don't. Sta-sta-stop."

Helen tried to meet Luciana's gaze, but her eyes kept rolling back into her head. She instinctively wrapped her legs around the woman and pulled her close as the dam burst at last. Wave after wave of pleasure crashed over her and she could feel her nails digging deep into Luciana's back even as her legs held the pulsing toy firmly inside of her.

She came to a shuddering stop at last, letting go of Luciana and laying back against the hardwood floor in exhaustion.

"Where have you been all my life?" she panted.

"That's not fair," Luciana laughed, kissing Helen gently then leaning down to whisper in her ear. "I've waited a lot longer than you!"

Chapter Twelve

"I suppose now I could show you how the house *actually* looks," Luciana sighed when the pair finally quit frolicking.

"What do you mean?" Helen propped herself up on one elbow.

"There's a glamor on the manor, to prevent you from… overreacting?"

Helen frowned, her brows coming together in a look that Luciana had no trouble interpreting.

"It's going to be a bit of a change," Luciana warned, raising one of her hands above her head.

"Let me guess, there's tacky, hundred-year-old wallpap-"

Helen's words trailed off as Luciana's hand began to glow. A faint purple beam of light shot out from her palm and hit the ceiling, where it spread out like an umbrella across the entire room. Everywhere the light touched the room *changed*. There were glowing symbols carved into the walls, motes of rainbow energy floating through the air, and the soft, smooth decor roughened to hewn stone, bronze wall sconces, and aged wood.

"Whoa," Helen gasped as she stood up and approached one of the walls. "The whole house is like this?"

"Most of it, yep."

"Wait a minute," Helen spun around. "So the stove *is* a big giant ancient looking cast iron stove?"

Luciana's laugh confirmed Helen's suspicions, and brought a slight pink back to her cheeks.

"Gods, you're observant."

"I *thought* I was hallucinating," Helen frowned. "Wouldn't be the first time. Perks of the crazy, I suppose."

"Sounds to me," Luciana approached her and tilted her chin up. "Like a superpower. After all, you saw the truth, right?"

Helen tried and failed to hide her smile.

"So, what is all this?" she ran her fingers across the wall. The symbols were bright and warm and crackled with energy at her touch.

"Runes," Luciana explained. "One of the True Languages."

"True Languages?"

"Remember when I told you there are several paths to magic? Well, these 'routes' were laid out by... well, in Fae lore, by the Gods. True Languages are the root of all modern speech, but they're... *more*. They're magic incarnate, they hold power beyond simply being letters and words."

"But there are others?"

"Many. Some Fae master only one, others try to learn them all."

"And you? Which one are you?"

"My focus is on the Runes," she shrugged. "Someone very dear to me - someone who helped to first cultivate my knowledge of magic - first introduced me many, many years ago."

"Ah," Helen felt a pang of senseless jealousy.

"Nothing like that," Luciana reassured her. "She was my mother, in so much as Fae actually *have* parents."

"You don't have parents?"

"Not in the traditional sense, no. But Fae can splinter off a portion of themselves, either by themselves or in pairs, trios, etc. The splinter is the closest thing you could compare to a Fae child."

"Are all Fae 'born' like that?"

"No, most of us are born sort of... spontaneously. When there's enough extra energy from fallen Fae, we coalesce into being."

"Like a star being born."

Luciana's eyes widened.

"I... suppose so, yes."

Helen turned back to the wall, studying the symbols more closely. They reminded her of fantasy novels and movies she'd seen.

"So your, erm, parent was some kind of... viking Fae?"

"Yes," Luciana's tone was becoming more clipped.

"So after you were born you just... left?"

"I spent a long time living with my parents," Luciana's brow furrowed. "But their goals and mine were not... compatible."

Luciana looked straight at Helen.

"I left, and I've never looked back."

"So you don't ever-"

"No," she interrupted. "Now come on, I'll show you the rest of the house - for real this time."

Luciana put an arm around her shoulders and steered Helen back to the staircase. The oddness of the staircase - and its seeming endlessness - seemed not to have changed at all.

When they got to the second floor, however, the glamor became much more obvious. The stairs felt *alive* now. The carved vines moved, and the petals of the stone flowers twitched slightly in some unfelt breeze. The baseboards around the house were lit with bright teal sigils, and the lights - which had appeared fairly normal before - had been replaced by glowing orbs of swirling light that floated unsupported in the air.

By the time they reached the library, Helen was fairly certain she was ready for anything - the chessboard corrected her line of thinking. Glowing, life-like replicas of each piece hovered just above the medallions on the ground. Each was fairly small, less than a foot tall, but exquisitely detailed.

The *shelves* were eye-catching as well. While the books looked the same, the shelves were absolutely covered in writing that zig-zagged this way and that, the symbols packed so closely together that they created a blur.

"What happened here?" she muttered to herself, running her hand across the wood.

The energy in the shelves felt like the push of a magnetic field, a cushion that repelled her fingers.

"You're not the only one who gets carried away."

Luciana's tone drew Helen's gaze, it was sadder than she expected.

"Come on, Helen, you must be hungry," she smiled and turned away. "Armand should be nearly done with dinner now."

Helen hurried to catch up as Luciana stepped away. She grabbed Luciana's hand and intertwined their fingers. Luciana didn't turn, but she gave Helen's hand a reassuring squeeze.

Luciana led the way back through the house in silence as Helen entertained herself by examining the changes to the architecture. They walked slowly, but it only took a few minutes for them to reach the door to the dining room. Helen was taken by surprise when Luciana, after opening the door wide, froze in the doorway.

"Helen."

Luciana's tone was unlike Helen had ever heard it. She sounded tense, even frightened.

"Helen, when you were in the garden, did you touch the roses on the hedge?"

Luciana's hand squeezed tighter until Helen's knuckles popped.

"Ow, you're hurting me," Helen yanked her hand back. "I-"

"Did you pick one of the flowers, Helen," she whipped around, her eyes wide. "This is-"

A banging caused both women to flinch.

The sound repeated, the unmistakable sound of someone pounding on a door so loudly that it echoed through the whole manor.

"Luciana, what is that?"

"Stay put, no matter what you hear."

Luciana waved one of her hands and the clothes she wore transformed to a long, elegant red dress. A crown of glowing spinning symbols adorned her brow and both of her hands glowed. She didn't look back, but headed straight for the exit.

Helen froze, alarm bells ringing in her head.

Told you so, it's all going to come crashing down.

"Be quiet."

You're probably about to wake up in a padded cell... again.

"Shut up," she hissed, her mind made up. "Shut up, shut up, shut up!"

Helen tiptoed as quickly as she dared, following Luciana as she made her way towards the front door of the manor. Luciana either didn't hear her or didn't care, but her long strides made it hard for Helen to keep up. She got far enough ahead that when Helen finally turned the last corner she could see the door was already open.

Three things became immediately apparent to her.

First, was Armand. He was sprawled out on the floor like a discarded doll, his blank expression overshadowed only by the fact that he was in several pieces. There wasn't any blood, just *pieces* of him, like some incomplete mannequin.

Second, Luciana was not alone. In front of her, just outside the threshold of the door, was a towering figure in a dark black suit. For all that it was dressed like a wealthy CEO - complete with cufflinks and a platinum tie clip - The *thing* was certainly not human.

It was built like a man, but it was deeply distorted. The being was easily nine feet tall, and was even slightly hunched over to peer in through the doorway. Long, gangly arms ended in long-fingered, over-large hands that hung down to the creature's knees. The legs were similarly thin and stretched, and the creature's body seemed disproportionately small by comparison. The head though, the head is what grabbed Helen's gaze and would not let go.

The creature - no, the *monster* - had an oval, almost egg-shaped head. The pale, whitish-gray skin was completely hairless, and held two deep black holes where its eyes should have been. It had no nose, but below the eyes was a mouth that Helen knew instantly she would see in her nightmares for the rest of her life. Dull, chapped, crimson lips stretched from one side of the head to the other. The mouth was so wide that Helen wondered if the whole head operated like a hinge when it was open.

Helen was certain she'd been soundless, she'd been so careful, but the moment her eyes landed on the creature, it turned those dark empty sockets in her direction and smiled. Dozens of yellowish, sharply pointed teeth appeared as those lips peeled back, and Helen felt a deep chill penetrate her body.

"Well, hello child," the thing spoke, and Helen caught a glimpse of a purple forked tongue. "Come closer, won't you?"

Helen felt herself straighten up. Entirely against her will she found herself moving forward as the thing crooked a long finger at her. She made it almost to the door before Luciana's arm shot out, stopping her in her tracks.

"That's close enough," Luciana growled. "What do you want?"

"So blunt," the creature's head didn't turn back. "Almost rude, one might say."

"Why are you here?"

"Well I'm just accepting your invitation, or don't you recall the last time we spoke?"

"I recall," Luciana frowned. "And *I* didn't invite you here."

"I see, then perhaps it was your... pet."

"She isn't a pet, and her invitation was unintentional," Luciana lifted her chin defiantly. "I'm sure she's glad you stopped by, but you'll no doubt understand her being unprepared for visitors."

"You speak for her?"

"This is *my* home."

"And yet you seem intent to question me, rather than welcome me as a guest."

"Oh far from it," Luciana replied. "A good host always desires to know her guests' desires."

"Are you then my host?" The voice was so hollow, but it *beckoned* with every word. "Perhaps I could come in."

"I'm terribly sorry but my only guest room is occupied by my friend here, and I simply couldn't have you over without a place to stay."

"And you?"

Helen's blood ran cold.

"May I have your name, child?"

"I-it's Hel-"

"I'm afraid she's using it," Luciana interrupted smoothly. "Perhaps when she's finished with it."

"Ah, what a shame."

"Helen, go back inside the house."

Helen looked down, shocked to see she was already past the threshold of the doorway. The monster in front of her, with its slick black armani suit and tight, pallid skin was just feet away from her, and certainly within reach.

"I-"

"She's enjoying our company," the thing reached out a long, gnarled finger and ran a dirty, jagged nail across Helen's cheek. "Aren't you enjoying our company?"

Helen felt sick. The nail was rough and jagged, and it burned her skin as it slid across the side of her face.

Be careful.

Helen cast a wide-eyed, sideways glance at Luciana, meeting the woman's gaze and noting the anger there. She drew a shuddering breath and opened her mouth to answer, then paused and reconsidered.

"I'm glad for company," she started slowly.

There is no debt, incur no debt!

"It is very, erm, pleasant."

"My guest is almost certainly famished," Luciana sidled over and put a hand on Helen's waist. "Regrettably, we were just sitting down to dinner when you called."

"Have I interrupted your meal?"

"Not at all," Luciana's hand tightened. "A simple delay, no harm done and no penance needed."

"Oh, but certainly I must make up for my rudeness," the creature smiled again. "You must allow me to repay the kindness of your time, Luciana."

"You are too kind," Luciana's tone hardened. "But I assure you *there is no debt.*"

Luciana's words caused the creature to jerk back in surprise, and a grimace of anger tinged the too-wide smile.

"I see, am I then unwelcome once more?"

"I'm afraid you've unintentionally accepted an accidental invitation, and I am unprepared for your visit."

"Then I suppose the polite thing would be to gracefully excuse myself."

Luciana said nothing, but her straight, defiant back, and hardened gaze showed no fear of the towering monster.

"Very well," its voice took on a low hiss. "Until we have the pleasure of meeting again, Luciana."

It shifted its body, now fully facing Helen.

"And you," the twin tongues licked the creature's lips. "I do hope to see *you* again soon."

Helen watched as the enormous man straightened up, his slender frame not unlike a massive, well-dressed scarecrow. He turned slowly, deliberately, and began to walk away. Her mouth popped open at his departure, because everywhere his foot touched there was a lingering, fog-like patch of pure darkness, which took several moments to dissipate.

By the time he stepped out of the light from the front of the house, he was already almost impossible to distinguish from the growing shadows outside their little circle of light. Helen wasn't sure exactly when she lost sight of him, but felt warmth return at last when she realized she could no longer see his lumbering frame.

"Luciana, what the fuck was that?"

"Come inside, Helen, and we'll talk."

The aesthetic changes in the house, which might've captivated Helen a few minutes ago, were now barely registering as she made her way to the dining room. Her eyes were drawn immediately to the rose bloom in the center of the table, the very rose she'd plucked from the hedgerow that morning. The wood around the rose was blackened and rotted, though the rose itself was still in pristine condition.

"I should've warned you," Luciana hung her head. "I should've told you not to toy with the hedgerow, or else I should've gone with you."

"I…"

Helen felt the energy in the room, and the simmering anger in Luciana. It reminded her of the less pleasant memories she had with her mother. Of

313

the times that the house quieted like a forest before a storm.

"That was my fault, wasn't it."

It was a statement, not a question, because Helen already knew the answer.

"There is no debt."

"That's a yes," Helen's hands clenched into fists. "Can you at least tell me what the hell is going on?"

"Have a seat," Luciana gestured at the table, before pulling out one of the gorgeous carved wooden chairs for herself. "We'll need something strong for this."

Luciana waved her hand over the table and two rocks glasses, complete with ice, appeared alongside a short, broad bottle of some ruby liquid.

"What's this?"

"Rosado," Luciana replied, uncorking the bottle and pouring half a glass in each cup. "It's rose wine. Fortified rose wine."

"What's *with* all the roses?"

"Different Fae express their power in different ways. It's an individual… signature, if you will."

"And yours is roses?"

"A perfect comparison. Beautiful from a distance, but strangling and sharp if you get too close."

"That's not the impression I get from you at all."

"Mmm," Luciana took a sip of the alcohol and nodded at the other glass. "Give it enough time."

Helen took Luciana's deep sigh as a chance to snake her hand out and grasp the icy cold glass in front of her. She lifted the drink to her nose and was delighted by the floral, sweet aroma. She took a sip and nearly choked, it burned like hell from her throat to the back of her nose.

"Jesus Christ, Luciana, you could use this for jet fuel."

The heat in her throat and nose subsided swiftly, replaced with a calming warmth within moments.

"The first sip is the harshest," Luciana gave her a weak smile.

"So," Helen prompted, cautiously trying another sip and finding her host was correct. "Who was that?"

"I don't know his true name, just like he doesn't know mine," Luciana replied. "I shudder to think what he would do if he did."

"Ok so, putting aside the true name thing, what do you *call* him?"

"The Smiling Man," Luciana grimaced. "He is a hunter. He's a monster, rightfully feared by all of our kind."

"A hunter?"

"In ages past, he discovered a secret of magic, a horrifying ability with world-changing ramifications," Luciana's gaze grew distant and her voice flattened. "He learned how to kill other Fae and *absorb* their energy, rather than allowing it to return to the balance."

"I thought Fae already absorbed the energy of the fallen?"

"We do - fairly, equally, and in small measure," Luciana drank deeply. "Much of the energy flows into the balance, where it becomes new Fae."

"So he just like, knows how to take *all* of it?"

"Yes," Luciana's knuckles turned white. "He learned how to kill our kind and consume them entirely, adding their power to his own."

"How, how do you fight something like that?"

"You don't, not anymore."

Helen's mind turned to the sketch she'd seen in Luciana's studio, and she felt her heart tremble at the water in Luciana's eyes.

"But you used to?"

"Yes," Luciana hung her head. "I was a hunter as well, Helen."

Helen gulped audibly.

"What, er, *who* did you hunt?"

"I hunted dragons. *We* hunted dragons. Dragons like The Smiling Man, who brought chaos, havoc, and ruin to not only the Fae Kingdoms but also to human kind."

"Wait, *that* was a dragon?"

"Dragons are so much more than humans imagine them to be," Luciana explained. "Dragons are what we call the Fae who choose to be outsiders so long that they lose all of their empathy. They lose the kindness and goodness that they may have once had, and they begin to covet nothing but death, destruction, and power."

Helen felt her face go pale and she took another fortifying sip of her drink.

"When a Fae isolates themselves, they begin to undergo a transformation. We need experiences, emotions, and interaction with others the way humans need food to eat or air to breathe," she continued. "Without that, we wither into cruel shades of ourselves."

"Why would anyone do that though?"

"As a Fae grows in power, the call of isolation grows stronger," Luciana finished her drink and poured another. "No one knows the cause of dragon sickness, only that it plagues all of us to some degree."

"Even you?"

"Even me," Luciana nodded. "That's why I keep Armand with me, to help me ward off-"

"Wait, oh my god, what about Armand?"

"He will be ok," Luciana smiled. "He is a construct, if you recall. He will reconstitute himself and join us before long."

Helen sighed with relief, her thoughts turning to the broken creation she'd seen by the doorway.

"So all Fae eventually succumb to the dragon sickness," she asked haltingly. "But there are hunters that what? Kill them when that happens?"

"Yes," Luciana nodded. "Long ago, it was a great problem."

"Why?"

"Because there were so many empty places in the world. There were many places to isolate oneself, places that are now filled with cities and towns. Manicured lawns have replaced prairies, and concrete covers the earth. It has become much harder to avoid the contact of others, even if you desire it."

"*You* found a place."

"I *made* a place."

Helen was silent for several minutes, content to drink the liquid that now went down smoothly. She could already feel a buzz in her head, but she was determined to know more.

"Why were you a hunter?"

"I was very good at it, I was a skilled warrior."

"Then why did you stop?"

"Someone dear to me died," Luciana chugged her entire glass and poured another. "She was killed."

"By him? By the Smiling Man?"

"Yes."

"The woman from the studio?"

"What?"

"The woman in the sketch," Helen clarified. "That's who you lost?"

"Askari, that was her name," tears welled up in Luciana's eyes but refused to drop. "She was killed right in front of me. She was *consumed* by that monster and there was nothing I could do about it. I'd killed before. Together we'd killed dozens of dragons, but this was different."

"So you stopped."

"I failed."

"I thought you said you couldn't lie?"

"What do you mean?"

"I mean, you didn't fail, you just didn't succeed, yet."

"You have a curious view of the world, Helen."

"My shrink calls that hallucinations," Helen tried in vain to elicit a smile.

Another moment of silence passed as the two women sipped their drinks.

Luciana appeared totally unaffected by the alcohol, but Helen was swiftly feeling its effects.

"What the hell is this stuff anyway?"

"I told you, fortified rose wine."

"Fortified how?" Helen blinked dumbly. "Because it's kicking my ass."

"Fortified with moon water," Luciana slid the bottle away from Helen and closer to herself. "And you should probably slow down."

"What about you?"

"I've been drinking this longer than your people have been on this continent," she snorted. "I'll be fine."

As if to prove her point, Luciana drained another glass and refilled it immediately.

"Luciana, what's a 'true name' mean?"

"Everyone has a True Name," she took a deep breath and let it out slowly. "Yours is Helen Marie LeFitte."

"How'd you know my-"

"Your mother picked up the phone and said 'LeFitte residence' before yelling your middle name."

"You were listening to my phone call?"

Helen felt anger rising inside of her at the thought of being spied on.

"It's not like that, Helen," Luciana raised her hands defensively. "I can sense *everything* that happens in this manor. Everything from the slightest breeze of a bee buzzing at the window to the creaking of the attic eaves in a strong wind."

Helen was not content with her explanation, but tried to lay down her hackles.

"Knowing someone's True Name gives you power over another," Luciana continued, her flushed cheeks the first indicator of the alcohol she was drinking. "*Especially* if you are Fae."

"What kind of power?"

"May I demonstrate?"

"Uhm, I guess so-"

"Helen," Luciana's voice was suddenly sweet as honey and utterly irresistible. "Helen, won't you please climb up on the table for me?"

Helen scrambled to get out of her chair, knocking over her glass in her haste, and heedless of the spilled wine. She practically jumped onto the table, desperate to please that silken voice.

"Helen," Luciana purred.

Helen realized, as if for the first time, the absolute beauty in the depths of Luciana's eyes. They were mercurial in their ability to defy description, but Helen was certain she'd be content spending the rest of her life trying.

"Helen!"

Helen snapped back to reality at Luciana's sharp tone.

She blinked in surprise, finding herself standing on one foot in a classical ballet pose in the center of the table, both arms out wide and her toes on pointe.

She wobbled a moment then crashed down to the table. Luciana lifted her glass, and the bottle, just in time to avoid it being spilled, and waited as Helen took her seat once more.

"That was excessive," Helen snapped. "And cruel."

"Sorry, Helen, I wanted to-"

"Oh don't worry, there is no debt, right?"

Luciana's mouth snapped shut and Helen felt a surge of joy at seeing her suddenly speechless.

What if she's done that before? What if that's all she's done since you got here? How can you trust her? You should leave. You should make sure this is real. The kitchen has knives-

"Shut up!"

"Excuse me?"

"I'm not talking to you," Helen glared.

"Helen, is something-"

"Wrong? Yes, something is wrong," Helen felt her passions rise. "You... you took advantage of me!"

"Helen, I wanted you to see how dangerous this is," Luciana looked down and swirled the liquor in her glass. "You must *never* give your name to the Fae."

"Well, mission accomplished."

Chapter Thirteen

Luciana continued to drink while Helen sat in sullen silence, the only sound in the room was the clink of ice on glass, and the pouring of the wine.

A tap at the door caused Helen's heart to race, but Luciana seemed utterly unphased.

"Madam, madam," Armand's soft voice was accompanied by a slight nod to each of them as he pushed open the door and entered. "Shall I serve dinner?"

"Yes, thank you, Armand," Luciana waved carelessly. "I'm glad to see you up and about again."

"My apologies for the delay madam."

Armand *looked* for all the world as though nothing had happened - as though he hadn't been torn to literal pieces less than an hour ago.

"He really is a construct," Helen shook her head in disbelief, surprise and wonder overcoming her irritation. "Just like you said."

"Yes, I built him to accompany me here, and I ensured he must be durable."

"In case someone came, like The Smiling Man?"

"Among other reasons," Luciana answered cagily.

"What other reasons?"

"Helen, I was *so* angry when I sequestered myself away," Luciana sighed. "I raged. I raged against the world, against the Fae, against my oath as a hunter. I could feel the dragon sickness growing in *me* of all people. *Me*, a dragon-slayer. For a time I... I needed an outlet. I-"

"You used him as a punching bag, didn't you," Helen whispered.

"I destroyed him, again and again," Luciana laid her head in her arms. "But I couldn't let him leave me, I brought him back every time and he forgave me. He forgave me *every time*."

Helen's anger cooled.

Here was a woman who was broken in her own right, and not so different from Helen. No doubt she shared some of the same struggles and fought the same demons. Helen finally saw past the flawless facade that Luciana had portrayed the last few days.

"I'm sorry," Helen reached out gingerly and rubbed Luciana's back. "I'm sorry that I have been blind to *your* pain because of my own."

"There is no debt," Luciana mumbled, but did not raise her head.

Helen felt herself on the edge of a similar breakdown. She could feel the crumbling edge of the dark and bottomless pit waiting in the back of her mind.

"Please, Luciana, let's have fun, let's not let that bastard ruin the whole night."

Luciana raised her head slightly, peering out at Helen.

"You still want to spend time with me?"

"Oh don't be so dramatic," Helen forced a smile. "Of course I do. You're always allowed to feel how you feel, or so my therapist says."

"I'll drink to that," she mumbled before draining her glass once again.

Helen eyed the bottle, now less than a quarter full, and then glanced back at Luciana. The woman's cheeks were flushed and her eyes, while still stunning, were starting to go a bit glassy.

"How about some food?"

"Right," Luciana straightened up and gave herself a small shake before clearing her throat.

"Armand?"

"Coming, madam," Armand's voice called out from the kitchen.

"Do you need help?"

"No, it's quite alright," the kitchen door swung open as he spoke, and he entered backwards with a pair of silver trays - one in each hand.

The tray in his left hand held plates of roasted vegetables, bowls of thick sauces, and steaming cuts of meat. In his right was a bowl of mixed greens, several small cups and bowls of ingredients like walnuts, strawberries, and various cheeses.

The man slid both onto the table effortlessly, positioning them perfectly before taking a bow.

"Shall I bring my lady something else to drink?"

"Another bottle of the Rosada Fortificado, please," Luciana emptied the last of their bottle into her glass and handed it to Armand.

"And you, madam?"

"I think water would be good," she glanced again at Luciana. "Maybe some coffee?"

"As you wish, ma'am."

Helen searched his eyes for pain, anger, any emotion at all. All she found was flat friendliness and impeccable professionalism.

"I shall return momentarily with your plates, flatware, and, of course, your drinks."

"Don't bother with the place settings, Armand, you've already outdone yourself."

Luciana accompanied her statement with a sharp knock, rapping her knuckles on the table with a bang. Place settings rattled into existence in front of each of them. The dishes were fine porcelain with gold trim and dark blue designs on them. Crystal goblets appeared at the head of their places, and shining brass flatware framed their plates.

"Wow."

"You ain't seen nothing yet," Luciana smirked. "Dishes are pretty easy. Compared to dragons anyhow."

Luciana stood, then reached out and grabbed a pair of silver tongs from one of the trays. She piled a sizable serving onto Helen's plate of each of the offerings. Grilled asparagus, roasted carrots, creamy mashed potatoes, and broiled brussels sprouts filled half her plate before Helen finally spoke up.

"I'm not actually that-"

"You need to eat," Luciana ignored her. "Being affected by magic takes a lot out of a human."

Luciana moved to the meat, selecting a chargrilled ribeye steak and placing it down gently on Helen's plate.

"Luciana, there's no way I can eat all of this," Helen protested. "It's going to go to waste!"

"You at least need some salad," the woman insisted, piling arugula onto the last open space and topping it with roquefort, cranberries, walnuts, and a drizzle of strawberry vinaigrette. "Please, for me?"

Helen frowned deeply.

She's bossy, see? She wants to control you like everyone else does. You should leave, you're better off on your own. She doesn't care about you.

She shook off her bad attitude as best she could while Luciana served herself. The food *did* look superb, and to be honest her mouth was watering already.

She picked up her utensils and gingerly cut into the steak. It was juicy, perfectly seared, and a stunningly even medium rare. Helen's first bite was enough to convince her that perhaps she *did* need some sustenance after all. The meat was heavily seasoned with garlic, chives, and butter, while the vegetables were loaded with rosemary, thyme, oregano, and paired well with a dark, thick balsamic vinaigrette from a small bottle on the tray.

"Do you really eat like this every day?"

"I do," Luciana mumbled through a mouthful before washing it down with another swig of her wine. "Food is an experience I can have, even here on my own."

"Why *are* you alone?" Helen sliced a brussel sprout in half and speared it with her fork. "Why not group up with your own kind, so you don't… er, succumb to dragon sickness or whatever?"

"I have no desire to be around my peers, all of whom either know of my failure or learn of it swiftly when I am near."

"People can't really blame you for not completing your mission, can they?"

"Wouldn't you?"

"No," Helen objected sternly. "No, I would recognize the weight and danger and difficulty of the task and I would understand-"

"What if you had failed?"

Helen paused, finding herself unable to lie and say she'd treat herself the same.

"I would... I would feel like you do."

"Like you'd failed?"

"Yes, like I'd failed."

"Like you do about school? About living on your own? About dealing with your mental heal-"

"Let's change the subject, please," Helen shrank down in her chair.

Luciana went quiet as well, aside from the gentle scrape of metal on porcelain.

"There are orders of Fae," Luciana offered at last. "A sort of quasi-governing body, if you will."

Helen said nothing, but her ears perked up.

"The Elders, all of whom know each other, set the laws for all Fae."

Helen met Luciana's eye, then looked down again.

"They do not change the laws lightly," Luciana continued. "I have never seen it done in my lifetime."

"Are they above the law?"

"No."

"Is The Smiling Man an Elder?"

"Not yet," Luciana frowned. "But it has been considered that perhaps that is his goal."

"What would happen if he consumed an Elder?"

"If an Elder lost to him in battle and was consumed, he could wreak havoc on a scale not seen in over millennia."

"So who is below the Elders, you?"

"There are three tiers of Fae below the Elders. There are the lenaí, the children; the fulloraðnir or 'those who've come of age'; and the doether or 'wisened ones.'"

"Which one are you?"

"I don't know," Luciana shrugged. "The field shifts, the balance shifts with it."

"Meaning what?"

"Meaning that Fae are categorized in how powerful they are compared to their peers, and I haven't interacted with my peers in decades."

"So you *could* be an Elder?"

Luciana laughed long and hard, a sound that brought some measure of joy back into the room.

"I'm not an Elder, of that much I'm sure."

"And you're not lenaí," Helen pushed. "Since you're obviously not a child."

"That is true. The lenaí are protected by the Laws of the Elders. No one can harm, hinder, or harass the lenaí, they must be allowed to grow into adulthood."

"But they can be mentored, or raised?"

"Yes, one or more Fae can parent a lenaí, but it often is a more communal effort," Luciana paused. "Unless one or more Fae purposefully come together to create a lenaí, called a lenaíaim. Then it is their child alone."

Helen set down her utensils and rubbed her temples, trying to absorb as much as she could of this woman's dangerous new world.

"Ok, Elders are mega-powerful, lenaí are children who can't be harmed," she listed them off on her fingers. "So you're either 'of age' or one of the 'wizened ones.'"

"Yes," Luciana nodded, taking a bite of her food.

"Well, which is it?"

Luciana frowned at her, but Helen was determined to get to the bottom of things.

"You're a... like a skilled gardener or plant witch or whatever, that's established," she started, her tone bordering on accusatory. "You can *clearly* do kitchen witching or whatever it's called."

"Helen..."

"You can 'sense' an entire manor, add a gym on command, and make a moving chess set, so that adds what, architecture witchery?"

"Helen, this conversation will not end well," Luciana's face was reddening, and for the first time Helen could hear her words start to slur. "Let's have dessert instead."

"I don't *want* dessert, Luciana!"

Luciana paused, shock obvious on her face.

"What *do* you want?"

"I want to know if we're safe, if *you're* safe," she shouted, pounding the table with her fist. "Is that fucking monster coming back here? What do we do if it does? If he tries to fight us, can you protect yourself? Protect me?"

Luciana set her glass down slowly during Helen's tirade, but waited quietly for it to end.

"I told you before," her tone was flat and even. "On these grounds, no one can hurt you."

"I can't stay here forever, Luciana! I have to go home, I have to go back to Tennessee and... and..."

What are we doing after that?

"I'm not saying you have to," she shot back. "The Smiling Man doesn't care about you, he cares about *me*, about our unfinished business that will someday end with his death or with mine."

"And you're sure when I leave here, I can just... just walk away, and none of this will follow me?"

"If that's what you want, yes."

"Luciana, answer me plainly," she straightened up. "Are we in danger, am *I* in danger?"

Luciana chewed her lip and pushed her food around her plate with her fork, stalling for time until Helen nearly burst.

"Yes, there is a potential that you are in danger."

Helen sat back, the sturdy wooden back of the chair supporting her as the wind left her lungs. She was here, in this gorgeous manor, eating this unbelievable food, and yet for all the opulence and shine and shimmer, she was no safer than she had been in her dorm room, unsupervised with a handful of pills and a bottle of whiskey.

Leave here, she's lying. All you have to do is leave...

"I can't."

"Helen, who is it you talk to?"

Helen's head jerked up, her eyes narrowed defensively.

"I talk to myself," she raised her chin. "Lots of people do-"

"I see," the corners of Luciana's mouth drooped into a frown.

Helen cast about for a distraction, uncomfortable with the direction she sensed the conversation was headed.

"So what kind of witch are you?" she blurted out as Luciana started to speak.

"What do you mean?"

"I mean, what can you do?"

"You want me to… to show off?"

"Unless you're too-"

Luciana interrupted her by sticking her hand out with a flourish, flicking her wrist, and creating an accompanying cracking noise. Streamers of blue sparkles burst out of thin air around the ceiling of the room, dancing and shining like a billion stars.

"Fireworks?" Helen goaded, her heart secretly dancing. "That's not quite as impressive as a new gym."

Luciana's eyes lit up and her smile widened.

"Alright," she cracked her knuckles loudly. "How about this?"

Luciana waved her hands again and this time the entire ceiling shifted - no, it wasn't the ceiling, it was the whole room! The dining room expanded, their table and chairs sliding sideways as the room pushed beyond the coverage of the floors above. Now twice as wide, the dining room was truly massive. The stone blocks that made up the ceiling twisted and crumpled into a fine dust that disappeared almost immediately. Every block that vanished showed a gaping hole all the way to the night sky. Once the roof was totally exposed, Luciana finished with a snap and a single, spotless pane of glass burst into existence to both cover the room and offer an uninterrupted view of the stars.

"Better?"

"Better," Helen stared in awe.

The stars above were bright and clear, save for some stray clouds that obscured about half of the sky. Somehow they looked so much *closer*, like she was on a mountaintop rather than the lowlands of Oklahoma.

"They're beautiful."

"In Fae lore, the stars are the original source of all magic," Luciana explained softly. "They are one of the entities to whom we pray - at least the Norse Fae do."

"Norse Fae? How do you mean?"

"It's like I said before," Luciana shrugged. "There are many paths to magic. Christianity, Shamanism, Shinto, Hinduism, the list goes on."

"But those are *human* belief systems."

"Yes, and it is the one true magic that humans possess," Luciana's tone grew solemn. "Humans *create* things through their faith. They create heavens and hells, monsters and saviors, angels and demons."

"So humans created the Fae?"

"The Elders believe humanity first gave us *form*, but did not create us. The first Fae were forged from the beliefs of your earliest ancestors. They took the forms of great bears, mammoths, and other terrors of the prehistoric world."

"And as we evolved new beliefs - new *legends*…"

"Yes, those legends became available to us, and our energy could take new forms. Now there are thousands of belief systems, all with their own versions of the supernatural, and all true in their own regard."

They sat in silence as minutes ticked by, both captivated by the night sky as dark clouds rolled past, hiding and revealing the stars as they went.

"It's almost perfect," Helen sighed.

"Almost?"

"Well, the clouds are-"

Luciana raised her hands, a soft white glow appearing in each palm and then spreading out and down around her arms, all the way to her elbows. She muttered something that Helen couldn't make out and then clenched her fists tightly. The glow flashed and winked out of existence but, high above them, a pin-prick hole appeared in the clouds.

The hole grew until all above the manor was clear of clouds, and all of the clouds rolling in slipped around the outside of the invisible window in the sky.

"Jesus, Luciana," Helen was nearly speechless. "That's incredible. I thought you were-"

"Just a kitchen witch?"

Helen looked over to see a sloppy grin on Luciana's face. She took another sip of her wine and set the glass down a little too hard, spilling some over the side.

"Luciana, I'm not one to judge-"

"Then don't."

Helen sighed, and considered holding her tongue, but there were too many red flags in her mind.

"Luciana, maybe you should switch to water," she said with a frown.

"Why, because I'm drunk?"

"Honestly," Helen shrugged. "Yeah, you're drunk, and it makes me nervous."

Luciana's laugh was colder than Helen had ever heard it.

"You think I'm dangerous?"

"Luciana, look at what you can *do*," she pointed at the sky. "Drunk you could do-"

"You don't know half of what I *could* do," Luciana shot back. "I'm not going to hurt you. You don't need to be nervous."

"Well, I am nervous, and I'd like you to respect that."

Luciana sobered up momentarily, fixing Helen with a bleary stare before straightening up in her chair.

"Right," she muttered, tapping the rim of her glass with a soft clink.

The deep red wine cleared instantly, replaced with an equal measure of water and ice cubes.

"Better?"

"Better," Helen's heart warmed a bit, and she couldn't help a faint smile that Luciana had listened to her needs.

"Come on," Luciana said more gently. "Let me show you that you don't have to be afraid."

The woman took a moment to grab a bite of food, then stood up again. This time, she held her hands low and at her side, then slowly began to draw them upward. As she moved the ground below them started to rumble with enough strength to set the dishes and windows rattling. A pair of shadowy columns appeared on either side of the broad glass roof, and it took Helen a moment to realize they were pillars of rock. As Luciana brought her hands together above her head, the columns all leaned inward and met above them, forming a perfect x-shaped pair of raw stone arches.

"Seriously, what *can't* you do?"

"Fae magic is driven by will and intention," Luciana's eyes had a wild gleam. "The stronger and clearer your intentions - and your *emotions* - the more you can accomplish."

"You um, light up when you do magic," Helen observed cautiously. "Is that... is that normal?"

"Magic runs deep in our blood," Luciana smiled in a fashion that Helen might've called nervously. "It's addicting, it's a powerful stimulant, and it invokes powerful... um, *reactions* in our bodies."

"And those reactions are different for all Fae?"

"Yes," Luciana stepped closer, waving her hand dismissively and sending the table sliding across the floor to clear the space between them.

"And for you?"

"Magic gives me a form of... pleasure, of excitement."

"Is that," Luciana was right in front of her now. "Um, is that because of-"

"It has to do with my previous forms," Luciana reached out and stroked Helen's cheek.

Rather than exciting her, Helen suddenly recalled The Smiling Man's touch, and she recoiled instinctively.

"Helen?"

"I'm ok," she took a step back, holding her cheek. "I just, I can't right now."

Luciana stayed put, though she was visibly restraining herself.

"You like the stars, yes?"

"What?"

Luciana's off beat question shook Helen from the recursive spiral in her mind.

"You've mentioned the stars several times now," Luciana clarified. "You like them?"

"I find them soothing, inspiring, and... magical."

Luciana nodded firmly, then raised her hands once more. She worked complex designs with her fingers and palms - both of which began to glow a soft golden light.

A swirl of silver and brown light began to spin on the ground between them. It grew broader, about two feet across, and then began to lengthen and raise itself up until Luciana was obscured by the tower of light.

The light disappeared with a crackle and Helen was suddenly standing in front of a massive telescope. The barrel of it was at least twelve feet long, with a lens at the end perhaps four feet across. She was directly in front of the viewing lens, and a pair of brass cranks were there to adjust her view.

"Good?" Luciana questioned, poking her head around the corner.

"I love it," Helen breathed, running a hand along the brass fixtures and stepping closer. "Luciana, this is insane, this is so complex and…"

She lied to you, just like they always do.

"And what?" Luciana grinned, obviously pleased with herself.

"And complicated," Helen frowned. "*Really* complicated."

Look above you, look in front of you, you could have left any time. She kept you here. She lied to you!

"Sh-shut up," she whispered to herself, taking a deep breath and clenching her fists.

"Helen?" Luciana raised an eyebrow. "Why not take a look?"

"No," Helen took two steps back, trying to regulate her breathing.

Ask her then. Make her tell you the truth.

"Helen, what's wrong?"

"Don't come near me right now," Helen held a hand up.

She could feel her heart beating out of her chest, it felt like it was going to explode. Her breaths were shallower than they should be - like someone was constricting her throat - and her head was pounding. She swallowed, trying in vain to alleviate the sudden dryness in her mouth.

"Window, door, table, fork-"

Telescope.

She closed her eyes and strained her ears.

"The wind, my breathing, clinking from the kitchen-"

Luciana's footsteps.

Helen snapped her eyes open to see Luciana approaching, and she instinctively took an equal number of steps.

"Helen, what-"

"No," Helen held her hand up again. "Just... just stop there."

"The smell of the food, the smell of the wooden floor-"

Her perfume.

"Shut up," she snapped loudly.

"Helen-"

"You too!"

Helen wiggled her toes and rubbed her hands together.

"My feet on the floor, the smoothness of my hands."

Taste is next, go ahead.

Helen looked up at Luciana, her stomach turning.

Go ahead, go crawling back.

Helen's gaze landed on Luciana's slightly parted lips.

"Helen," Luciana looked so confused, so innocent. "I'm worried…"

Liar.

"Luciana, I need you to answer something."

"Of course, anything."

"Could you have fixed the bridge?"

"Helen, I-"

"Could. You. Have. Fixed. The bridge?"

Luciana paused, her shoulders slowly dropping.

"Yes, but-"

"And my car?" Helen ground her teeth. "Could you have fixed my car?"

"Yes."

Helen was clenching her jaw so hard she could feel a spiking pain up to her eardrums.

"Why?"

Luciana didn't answer, but looked down at the floor.

"Why did you keep me here, if you could have let me go at any time?"

Luciana's back straightened, but she still didn't speak.

"Answer me!"

"I couldn't have just magiced your car back and fixed the bridge," Luciana snapped. "That wouldn't have made any sense to you when you woke up!"

"So? Who cares!"

"So, I couldn't just reveal myself to you as Fae, it is against our laws!"

"But as soon as I knew," Helen pointed a finger at her. "As soon as I knew, you could have made it happen. I could've gone home!"

"Did you really *want* to?"

"You don't get to tell me what I want!"

Helen was screaming now, her fists clenched hard by her sides.

"Helen, I'm sorry that I-"

"You think I want your apology? You kept me here for *days* without my medication. Medication you *knew* I needed! You kept me from going home, from... from getting back to my life!

"I *am* sorry, Helen," Luciana stepped back. "I never intended to keep you here, but you... you fascinate me, you make me smile and you make me feel things that I haven't felt in-"

"Luciana, I am not the cure for *your* loneliness," Helen growled. "I am my own person!"

"Yes, you are, and I'm sorry to have treated you otherwise," Luciana looked down. "I was selfish and wrong, and I wish desperately that I could take it back and choose better - with your interests in mind and not my own."

Helen balked, she wasn't used to genuine apologies and this one was taking the wind out of her sails more quickly than she cared to admit.

"I don't want to speak to you anymore tonight, maybe ever," Helen stood stock-straight and defiant. "May I go now?"

"Go where?"

"Home."

"Helen, I will not keep you, but it is late and dark and you've been drinking," Luciana pleaded. "Will you please wait until morning?"

Helen wrestled with herself. What Luciana said was true, and aside from being buzzed, she was quite tired.

"I'm sleeping in my own bed, in my own room."

"Of course-"

"And I don't want to see you in the morning."

"...of course.

Chapter Fourteen

Helen tossed and turned.

Her sheets and blankets were tangled hopelessly and she'd been trying for what felt like hours to go to sleep, but Luciana's betrayal would not let her rest. She fumed, playing over the events of the last few days with a frustrating mix of gratitude, anger, resentment and desire.

She saved your life.

"Who's side are you on?" she rolled over once more, covering her face with a pillow.

The pillow didn't help, in fact it carried the sweet vanilla and cinnamon scent of Luciana directly to her nose. Her mind returned instantly to their bodies entwined, to the pleasure she'd-

"No," she sat up and threw the pillow across the room where it hit the door with a dull thump.

"Fuck," she put her head in her hands. "What the fuck are you doing Helen?"

She reached for the side table out of habit, but stopped herself short.

"You don't *have* a phone, dumbass."

Thanks to her.

She peered through the darkness instead, looking for the faint face of the clock on the wall. The ivory backboard made it difficult, but not impossible to read.

"Three a.m.," she sighed.

The sun will be up soon.

Helen lay back on the bed once again, her eyes wide, staring at the ceiling. The plaster had small whorls and ripples, as many old plaster walls did, and she focused on them until-

Oh, now you want me?

Helen didn't answer. She allowed herself to sink into the mattress below her body, to pull back from reality until her hurt feelings were… nothing. Until all feeling was gone, and her existence was that of a casual observer.

Careful now, wouldn't want to get too comfortable again would you?

Helen could feel her heartbeat slowing, her breath steadying, and her pupils widening. The patterns on the ceiling started to move, and Helen smiled. She watched them dance and spin in mesmerizing chaos. When they moved the wrong way, she nudged them with her mind, pushing them back into order. Time passed and the moon followed its course across the sky, casting new shadows on her playground.

Helen incorporated the shadows into her vision, bending and molding them to her purposes. Her doctors - those who she'd confided in - called these hallucinations, delusions, or her personal favorite, "disturbed cognitive function."

She just called it safety.

Her medicine suppressed the sights, sounds, and feelings, but when she was unmedicated or when things got really intense in her life, they always came back. It'd taken her years to figure out she could influence them sometimes, and years more to realize that they weren't "normal."

Now, they were a good indicator that she needed to get closer to people she trusted, that she needed to start examining herself and her actions as best she could, and that she needed to revisit her safety plan.

Helen groaned at the thought.

Her safety plan, a present upon exiting her last in-patient stay, was an obnoxious document meant to give key people indicators to look out for in case she couldn't or wouldn't tell them she was entering an episode. It was also intended to keep her from doing anything too damaging to her reputation, her finances, or her life.

Luciana doesn't know it. She wouldn't know what to look for.

"So?"

You could do anything, she wouldn't be able to stop you, would she?

Helen suppressed a shiver and ignored the thought. She needed to sleep, and the sooner the better.

Helen awoke to a sunbeam shining directly on her face. She must've managed a little sleep, though just how much remained to be seen.

She rolled over, clearing her face of the blinding light, and straightened the glasses still on her face.

"Hmm," she frowned. "Eight."

That tracked with the lowness of the sun on the horizon. She sat up and stretched widely, freezing in place upon seeing a note atop a pile of folded clothes at the end of the bed. She recognized the clothes of course - it was the outfit she was wearing when she'd arrived here at Casa De Rosas.

The note was a single piece of paper folded in half, with Helen's name written in sprawling, gorgeous handwriting. Helen reached out and picked it up gingerly. Nothing happened. She must've stood there for more than a minute, weighing the thought of opening the letter, but in the end she tossed it to the side, unopened.

She slipped out of her borrowed pajamas and into her jeans, t-shirt, and unbuttoned flannel. She was surprised to see that even her sneakers were there, immaculately cleaned and dried, ready for wear.

Perhaps you owe Armand a thank you.

"I don't owe either of them anything," she snapped. "There is no debt, remember?"

Five minutes later, she was lacing up her sneakers and headed for the door.

Her hand hovered over the heavy silver handle, and a thousand scenarios of what she might find on the other side played through her mind.

Well?

Helen reached out, twisted the handle, and jerked the door open, half expecting Luciana to be there waiting. Instead, she was greeted with a silent, empty hallway. Her sneakers seemed over-loud on the wooden floors, and she tentatively worked her way toward the landing.

Luciana's bedroom door was shut tight, and though Helen paused a moment, she couldn't hear anything from the other side. She slipped down the stairs to the library, noting that the chessboard had been reset, and crept toward the front door.

Skulking around in the shadows, how appropriate.

She stood up defiantly, ignoring the prompting in her mind.

By the time she made it to the entrance, she was beginning to question whether or not Armand and Luciana were real people at all. She thought back to the note still laying on the bedroom floor above, but refused to turn around.

Unseasonably warm air and a soft breeze greeted her when she finally summoned the strength to head outside. She let go of the handle without a backwards glance and took two steps out onto the stone, letting go of the breath she hadn't realized she was holding. She stood there, waiting for the sound of the door shutting behind her.

Even though she was prepared for it, she was still startled by the unsettling empty boom of the door swinging shut.

"Here we go," she muttered to herself.

Helen stepped off, making her way down the path toward the bridge - or at least according to her memory that's where she was headed. Thankfully, her memory served her well and, after a few minutes of walking, she turned a corner past a particularly large flush of flowering bushes and not only the bridge, but also her car came into view.

Her vehicle looked as clean and pristine as it had the day it was driven off the lot - long before she'd ever owned it. She jogged the last few dozen feet, her eyes wide with surprise. She ran her hand across the fresh paint, up the corner of the trunk and along the top of the small silver sedan as she approached the driver's side door.

Looking through the uncracked glass she could see her keys, complete with all of the clutter and tchotchkes, from her two week sobriety chip to her tiny silver alicorn charm.

"I'll be damned," she pulled the handle and the door popped open smoothly. "Honest about something at least."

Did she ever really lie to you, or are you being-

"I'm not going to gaslight myself," she announced loudly, taking her seat and turning the key. "She said I was *stuck here,* and that was a *lie.*"

Did she?

The engine purred to life as a glare settled on Helen's face and she set about adjusting the mirrors. She was arranging the rearview when she realized that all of her luggage was there just as she'd packed it when she left the university.

"Wait."

She twisted around, grabbing her olive drab canvas backpack and pulled it into the front seat. Unclipping the flap that held it closed, she pulled out a plastic bag of clear orange bottles.

"Venlafaxine, Bupropion, Lithium, Trazodone, Prazosin, Melatonin, Sumatriptin," she counted each off, rattling them to ensure they weren't empty.

She cast a glance at the stainless steel water bottle on the side of the backpack, then back to her medications, but ended up tossing the backpack and the bag of medications into the passenger seat and settling herself into the driver's seat instead.

With a deep, heavy sigh she put the car in drive and gently pressed the gas. The car crunched across gravel as she approached the broad wooden bridge before her. She tried to shake the feeling that she'd snap the bridge in half and plunge once more into the deep cold waters. Her car crept right up to the edge before she hit the brakes. The car jerked to a stop and Helen hung her head.

"Come on," she murmured. "It's a normal, perfectly steady bridge."

That was broken yesterday.

"Quiet you."

Helen closed her eyes, took a steadying breath, then snapped them open and floored it. Her zippy little sedan barely broke twenty miles per hour by the time she hit the other side of the bridge, rumbling onto the narrow, backcountry road beyond.

"*In seventeen miles, turn left.*"

Helen nearly jumped out of her skin, her head whipping around to look into her passenger seat again.

She lifted the backpack and tore through it until she found her phone tucked into a side pocket, full of charge, and with her address still plugged in to the navigator.

A little of the wind flew out of her sails and she glanced back behind herself. The property looked different now, like just another thick, old-growth forest with no sign of the manor within. The bridge was the only man made feature in sight, sitting some six feet above a tranquil river. It took more effort than she cared to admit, but she was finally able to tear her eyes away from the rearview and back to the road ahead.

She hit the gas and started up the slightly inclined gravel path, eager to leave this place, and her aching heart, behind her.

Again.

The next seventeen miles flew by without incident, aside from some skidding caused by Helen taking unfamiliar curves too quickly, and she found herself at a tee-intersection where the gravel met a poorly maintained asphalt two-lane.

Taking a precautionary look back at her phone, she confirmed that she was indeed headed left, and pulled out onto the much smoother surface. Every minute of silence was another minute of self-doubt, anger, and frustration playing in the echo-chamber of her mind, so it wasn't long before she tapped the power button on the car's radio.

Solid country gold poured out of her speakers and she cranked the volume dial until she couldn't even hear the rushing wind outside anymore. Pulling her hand back, she realized the button she'd broken in her outburst was now fixed, no longer jammed in as a reminder of her temper. She ran her finger across it, and smiled. Of all the buttons on the display, she'd managed to break the 'pause' button.

"Classic."

She roared down the blacktop going ninety-three for the next hour, unsure exactly what unlabelled highway she was on but convinced from the position of the sun that she was going North by Northeast. The road was a little bumpy, but it was also nearly straight and completely, utterly devoid of other drivers.

"In two miles, take the exit on the right."

"Right-o," Helen tapped the brakes, bringing herself down to a more manageable seventy by the time the interchange came into sight.

She crested a low hill and found herself preparing to merge onto I-40, which would take her straight back to Tennessee. To Nashville. Home.

She slowed to forty-five and pulled out onto the exit ramp, both hands clenching the steering wheel with white knuckles and a grim look of determination on her face.

What a waste. But then again, who'd be surprised?

The blaring of a semi's horn snapped her back to reality and she swerved. Realizing she was at the end of the merge lane, she gunned it to get in front of the tractor trailer rapidly approaching from her rear.

"Get it together," she mumbled, catching up to highway speed.

A sudden flood of chimes went off from her phone as she re-entered better service, so she reached over with her free hand and glanced at the screen. Her voicemail was full, which wasn't exactly uncommon, and she could see a number of missed calls from the past few days - including more than a dozen from her mother.

You'll be hearing about this-

"Forever," she cringed. "I know."

Her mother was going to be an entirely separate problem, and one that Helen didn't really want to think about.

You might as well, you'll be dealing with her soon enough.

Helen chewed her lip, subconsciously brainstorming ways to explain how her car - which she'd insisted was totalled - was now in pristine condition, along with all of her personal effects, and her completely functional cellphone.

As if summoned from her mind into reality, the small device started to ring the high-pitched, jarring tone that meant her mother was calling. She confirmed the caller on her car's dashboard, and moved instinctively to send her to voicemail. Her finger hovered over the decline call button for a long moment, before she let out a resigned sigh and hit accept.

"Helen?"

"Yes, mom."

Who else would it be?

"Helen, I can't help but notice you're answering your *cell phone*."

"Mom, I-"

"Is it safe to assume you have rescued it from the river then?"

Helen grit her teeth, but didn't respond.

"Helen, I can hear you driving," her mother's exasperated sigh was oscar-worthy. "So don't bother telling me you're losing signal."

"I wasn't going to, mom," Helen retorted sharply.

"Are you headed home?"

"Yes."

"And did you borrow a car, or did you manage to rescue that as well?"

"Mom, can we not?"

"So you're sticking to your story then, that your car was destroyed in a flood or whatever?"

"It wasn't a flood, I had an accident and my car went into the-"

"Into the river, yes, you told me," her mother paused, spiking Helen's anxiety. "Helen, I need to ask you a serious question."

"Ok?"

"Are you off your meds?"

"Dammit mom, why is that always the first thing you ask me?"

"Because you spent three weeks in a psychiatric ward, and I only found out you were there because they weren't sure you'd wake up from that *coma* you were in."

"Mom, I told you-"

"No, Helen, I'm telling you," she could feel her mother's anger through the phone. "I'll be damned if I lose my daughter to her own selfishness!"

Silence followed her outburst, and Helen struggled internally - her mind a pendulum swinging between guilt and anger.

"So?"

"So what, mom?"

"Are you *medicated*?"

"No, I haven't had my medication in a few days," Helen tried to keep her tone as neutral as possible. "I told you, the-"

"The river, yes, right. Well, you know my rules, Helen, you're not going to stay under my roof unless you take your medication."

"Mom, I didn't stop taking it on purpose!"

"Helen, I want to believe you, I really do."

"Then *do*."

"Do I need to remind you how we got to this place? How you... went off the deep end?"

"Mom-"

"Threw away your scholarships, drank yourself half to death, how you-"

"Mom!"

"And let's not skip past the pills, which you nearly *died* from."

"Well, that was kinda the point, wasn't it!"

Helen heard her mother's sharp intake of breath through the phone.

"When can I expect you?" she finally said, her tone frosty.

"I'm about," she glanced at her screen. "Seven and a half hours away."

"Very well. I'll leave dinner in the oven then, unless you're eating on the road?"

"I'll grab something on the road, mom, you don't need to worry about it."

"Hmm."

Helen cast a frustrated glance at the screen.

"What?"

"Nothing."

"Jesus, mom-"

"Don't take the Lord's name in vain," she snapped.

"You obviously wanted to say something, mom," Helen hissed. "Or you wouldn't have made that sound."

"Well, you just need to be careful how much of that junk food you eat," the woman's flippant tone grated on Helen's nerves. "You've gained some weight from those medications you know, and it's not going to the most flattering places."

"Wow, thanks, mom."

"Don't be mad at *me*," she huffed. "Heaven forbid I look out for my daughter's health and welfare."

"I'm capable of doing that for myself, thanks."

Helen's right hand instinctively went to her stomach. She felt the slight puff where her stomach folded and felt a flush of shame. She tightened her belly, sucking in as best she could, and was only marginally rewarded with a slightly smaller pooch.

She's right. You're getting fat.

"I'm a healthy weight."

"Oh alright, you kids have redefined 'healthy' so much at this point I suppose it applies to everyone."

"Mom, you're being fatphobic."

So are you.

"Oh please, phobic this and phobic that. I have a gay daughter, don't I?"

"That doesn't actually excuse-"

"And I've never said a cross word about your lifestyle, have I?"

"It's not a lifestyle-"

"Besides, your father was chubby, and I loved him enough to make you."

"Well, that settles it," Helen rolled her eyes.

"Helen, I'm begging you," her mother's sudden emotion made Helen pause. "Take your medication."

Helen glanced over to the passenger seat, making eye contact with the bag of pill bottles there.

"Did you hear me?"

"Yeah mom, I heard you."

"Helen, you know I do love you, more than anything."

"I love you too, mom," Helen swallowed the lump in her throat. "I'm uh, I'm gonna go though, maybe listen to some music, ok?"

"Drive safe."

"Thanks mom."

She tapped the end call button, feeling as she always did after speaking to her mother - conflicted.

"Is this really what I'm going back to?"

Well, if you hadn't failed in the first place.

Helen's thoughts turned back to her freshman year. She'd been driving this very highway, and headed further west than she'd ever been. She was so energetic, so *happy*.

What had happened?

You couldn't handle it.

She'd been flying high on a full-ride scholarship in mathematics - no easy feat - and excited to finally be away from home. She'd been just about as excited as a young woman could be, freshly out of the house for the first time and ready for a life of independence.

And what did you do with that freedom?

"Threw it all away," she sighed.

Her freshman year had gone well, or well enough at least. Straight A's in the fall turned to B's and C's by the middle of her Sophomore year. Shortly thereafter, the stress had started to build. Her worldview started to fracture as the obsessively clean, strictly regimented lifestyle of her mother started to fall apart in the presence of so many new ideas and minds. Not to mention the presence of so much alcohol.

And so many drugs.

She cringed, remembering not-so-fondly the first time she'd done acid. She hadn't known what it was at the time, only that she was drunk and that her girlfriend at the time had slipped something into her mouth and told her to *"enjoy"*.

What followed was a six-hour nightmare that ended with her locking herself in a closet and sobbing uncontrollably. Thankfully, she was discovered by a pair of young women who babysat her through the rest of her trip. She *ought* to have learned her lesson there, but she didn't.

Do we ever?

"No."

Helen tried to pinpoint exactly *where* things had gone off the rails, and why.

In all honesty, she'd been experiencing anxiety for years before she left home, depression, too. She'd only held it together because of how tightly controlled her home had been. There was no room for deviation in the LeFitte household. Anything outside the norm, outside of the expected, was to be contained, controlled, and buried far for the light of day.

The unexpected freedom of being away from that prison uncovered just how much she'd tried to suppress. Traps that had been buried throughout her life rose to the surface, and she suddenly found herself standing in the middle of a minefield.

It was only a matter of time until one went off.

For a while she kept it together. She self medicated with alcohol, pot, shrooms, just about anything she could get her hands on. Of course, six months later she was doing lines of coke off of a sorority girl's chest on the tail end of a six day bender.

She rode the high as long as she could, ignoring the fact that the wheels were falling off mid-ride. When the crash came - and it *did* come - it hit like a freight train. She was drunk and or high for the better part of six straight weeks, and when that didn't get her out of the hole she was in, she ended it with a bottle of acetaminophen with codeine.

Well, not 'ended,' exactly.

Helen groaned, no amount of therapy was going to remove the guilt and shame she'd felt when she woke up in a hospital bed to see her mother crying. It was the rawest emotion she'd ever seen from the woman, then or since.

Her therapists, and there had been many, had been a subject of some debate between her and her mother. In the eyes of Janice LeFitte, Helen didn't *need* therapy. She just needed self discipline and pharmaceuticals. Exactly how pills were better than therapy was something Helen still didn't understand, but her mother had been more than supportive of the idea. So much so that she regularly commented that Helen needed to wean herself off of her therapists, focus on her medication, and practice more self control.

So we're going back... why, exactly?

"Because," Helen paused, chewing her bottom lip.

A car horn snapped her back from contemplation and she jerked the wheel to the right, coming to a rolling stop on the shoulder. She calmed her quickened breath and looked up, locking eyes with herself in the rearview mirror.

"Because I *should* go back," she whispered. "Right?"

Helen thought back to the last few days, struck suddenly by the overwhelming *support* she'd felt - and how that contrasted with the welcome she could expect back home. She couldn't deny that her heart lifted when she thought of Casa De Rosas, even despite the revelation that Luciana had misled her.

So you admit it?

"Fine, she didn't *lie*," Helen frowned. "But she wasn't honest either."

She seemed remorseful though.

"That doesn't mean she deserves a second chance."

You've given more chances to people who've treated you worse.

Helen sighed, her mind wandering uncontrollably to the nights they'd spent together, to the fiery once-in-a-lifetime passion she'd found with this wild, impossible woman.

"Fuck," Helen closed her eyes, then rubbed her temples. "Fuck, fuck, fuck."

A deep breath in - followed by a slow breath out - did absolutely *nothing* to slow her climbing pulse and racing mind. Her eyes opened back up, and she found herself staring into the mirror once again.

Do it.

She reached up and grabbed hold of the rearview, snapping it off with a yank and a twist, and throwing it over her shoulder into the backseat. She checked her side mirrors, then punched the accelerator to pull a gravel-spraying u-turn across the median before heading back the way she'd come.

Chapter Fifteen

The trip back had started well, but now Helen was on backroads that looked anything but familiar.

"Dammit," she growled. "I know this is the way I came."

Unless none of it was real, of course.

Helen ignored the voice inside her head, pushing onward instead. She paused time and time again to check her phone, but none of the roads matched exactly what she remembered. She was on the right road, or at least the right two-lane, but there just wasn't anything that looked familiar. In fact, she wasn't seeing any side roads at all.

She took a deep, calming breath, and pulled over onto a slightly wider section of gravel-covered shoulder.

"Ok," she reassured herself. "Look around, *something* has to be familiar, right?"

She studied the roadside around herself, willing it to give her the answer she was looking for. She'd surveyed just about everything in sight -

and nearly given up - when she happened to look off to her right.

"No way."

The gravel she'd pulled over on, which she thought was simply a wider section meant for turning around, actually *continued* into the brush. It looked familiar, but also much more… overgrown than she recalled from the morning.

That can't be it, there's too much grass in the gravel, the whole road looks abandoned.

Helen shoved her doubts aside and performed a quick three point turn, reorienting herself so she was pointed down the narrow gravel path.

"So much for the fresh paint job."

The road was considerably bumpier than it had been a few hours ago, and Helen felt a growing sinking feeling in the pit of her stomach. Weeds had sprouted up all over the road, if it could even be called that anymore, and tree branches that had been nowhere near the road now obscured her vision and scraped along the sides of her small car.

Still, with every mile, she was more and more certain that she was on the right path. More features of the terrain looked familiar, and a subtle tug in her heart told her she *must* be going the right way.

She held out hope through the drive, forcing herself to reframe every sign of abandonment as a clever disguise to keep out intruders, but when she finally got to the bridge across the river, she felt the crushing weight of reality.

The bridge was a worn, half-rotted wreck, and the hedgerow of rose bushes on the other side was a massive wall of brown, dead, leafless vines and thorns.

"Fuck," she cursed as she rolled to a stop just before the bridge.

Way to go, missed your chance.

Helen frowned, then, before she had a chance to second-guess herself, she unclipped her seatbelt and hopped out of the car. She shoved the door shut as she walked forward, making a beeline for the side of the bridge that looked least damaged.

She tapped her foot on the first beam and found it surprisingly sound. The next one creaked a bit, and the third let out a nerve-wracking groan, but they all held her as she picked her way across the river.

When Helen landed on the other side at last, she let out the breath she'd been holding and said a silent thank you to whoever had been looking out for her. She turned to the hedgerow and walked through the archway onto the manor's grounds. The archway was half-covered in vines but there was still plenty of room for Helen to slip through to the other side.

Waist-high dead grass, clumps of dead wildflowers, and the remains of dozens of trees and shrubs met her gaze and nearly brought tears to her eyes. Without the leaves and foliage in the way, she could see the upper floor of the manor above the tops of the dead and dying plants. The building had a cracked and broken roof, the windows were mostly missing their glass, and the paint on the outside was peeling badly.

Helen jogged through the remains of the gardens to the main entrance of the house and gaped at the damage wrought since the morning. This building was certainly the one she'd been living in, but it looked like it hadn't been touched in a century. The whole structure was damaged by wind, rain, and time.

Even the main door was only hanging on by a single hinge.

"Luciana," she shouted impulsively. "Luciana, are you here?"

Nothing.

Helen approached the entrance. She considered knocking, but it seemed like it would be a moot point so she simply yanked the stubborn door open and stepped inside. Her eyes were still adjusting to the darkness inside, but she could see Armand's outline just ahead.

"Oh thank god," she walked over and embraced the figure, only to find it hard and unyielding.

"What the hell?"

She pushed the man out to arm's length to get a better look. It was definitely Armand, but rather than a human being he was a crudely carved wooden mannequin dressed in moth-eaten dress clothing.

Armand was gone too?

Probably your fault.

Helen ran past the mannequin and skidded to a stop in the library. All of the books were gone and the chess board on the floor looked like it had been abandoned mid-game. The kitchen was a dusty mess, and it looked like a family of mice must've moved in at some point. The art gallery was just as empty as the library, which Helen took as a good sign - the art and the books didn't remove themselves, right?

She headed upstairs, cracking open the door to Luciana's master suite first. Everything looked like she'd last seen it, except the clothes in the closet were gone and there was a thick layer of dust on everything.

"Damnit," Helen chewed her fingernail, racking her brain. "There's got to be a way."

Not necessarily. You left, remember?

Helen got an idea and headed for Luciana's studio.

The door was in fairly good shape, and so was the room beyond. Nearly everything was gone, but there was one rolled up painting sitting on a dust-covered table. The room had no windows, and there certainly wasn't any power in the building, so Helen grabbed the canvas and brought it back out into the hallway before unrolling it.

She recognized it immediately.

Helen gently traced her finger across the lines, holding her breath and fighting back the urge to cry. It was the painting Luciana had made of her, and unlike everything else in the mansion, it seemed totally unaffected by the ravages of time.

"Dammit, Luciana," she whispered, rolling it back up and trying not to squeeze it too hard.

Maybe she left us something else.

Helen perked up, then practically sprinted back to "her" room down the hall.

This room was particularly damaged, and there were leaves and broken window panes all over the floor. Helen shuffled around, looking this way and that until she finally peeked under the bed and found what she was looking for.

The time-yellowed piece of paper was still folded, and still bore Luciana's sprawling signature. She sat on the edge of the bed and flipped it open.

My Dearest Helen,

I want you to know that I recognize that I have no excuse for my actions. I know it was wrong to mislead you. I haven't felt a connection to another being the way I did to you in so long. I acted selfishly, and I am truly sorry. I wish I could repair what we had, I wish I could magic away my stupidity and my rudeness. But magic doesn't work that way, and it wouldn't be fair even if it did.

We only spent a few days together, but you have impacted me greatly. You reminded me that there is life outside of the protected, closed off world that I have built here.

You reignited my passion, you rekindled my love of art, you gave me a reason to cook again, and dance again, and to look beyond myself. I am leaving you the painting that I made for you, as I believe it should belong to the muse who inspired me to make my first work of art in over a century. In the dresser drawer in your room, I am also leaving you the deed to this manor, complete with applicable signatures.

I will have no further need of this home, as you have inspired me to break free of the prison I created and to re-engage with a new and exciting world. I apologize that when my magic leaves this place it will be a victim of time once more, but I hope that the value of it outweighs any frustration it might cause.

I'm not sure you'll ever read this letter, and I couldn't blame you if you didn't, but I wish you all the best in life. I wish you healing, and peace, and

passion, and selfless love. Most of all, I hope to see
you again someday, in this life or the next.

Yours with love,

Luciana De La Rosa

The letter had the imprint of a kiss in the lower corner of the paper, marked in dark, heavy lipstick. Helen brushed her thumb across it and her features fell as part of the ancient makeup crumbled away.

"Fuck," she hung her head and let the letter fall to the floor.

A gust of wind whistled through the broken pane at her back and sent the note skittering across the floor. Helen popped up and chased it across the room, catching it just before it slid under the dresser. She straightened up and reached out a trembling hand to the top drawer. Pulling it open, she uncovered a fine leather folio, thick with documents.

Helen plucked it out and flipped through it. She didn't understand any of the legal jargon but the gist seemed to be that Luciana had indeed left her the whole property, which apparently encompassed almost 60 acres. She wanted to be excited. She wanted to be overjoyed that she'd suddenly inherited what probably amounted to a fortune.

But all she felt was disappointment.

She set the folio back, and set her letter on top of it before sliding the drawer shut again and heading back out of her room. She made it to the stairs, pausing at the landing, and staring aimlessly at the stone. The carvings were still exquisite, but the magic was gone. The *pull* was gone.

Helen looked upward, tempted to go examine Luciana's old workspace, but headed downward instead. She found herself back in the library, running her hands along the faded wood and plaster walls as she headed for the main entrance.

When she stepped outside at last, the sun felt a little less warm. The sky above was still clear, but there was a growing shadow of clouds on the horizon and the winds were picking up. She stood numbly for several minutes, staring out at the overgrown mess of a property around herself and feeling the same wild, chaotic energy building in herself.

Well then, center yourself, idiot.

Helen took a deep breath and tried to concentrate on calming herself down. A pair of birds cawed in the distance, the wind whistled loudly through cracked window panes, and a woodpecker in the distance was beating a sharp staccato against some poor tree, all of which sought to disrupt her calm. Her brow furrowed and her jaw clenched until it hurt, finally pushing her to give up. This place was *not* the peaceful haven it had been, and Helen was unlikely to find peace here anymore.

She headed for the gravel path that would take her to her car - and back home - but paused when she hit the fork in the path. She was suddenly reminded of the greenhouse, of the koi in the pond and the peace she'd felt there.

Surely *something* had to be left of the greenery there, right?

Her feet carried her past scrubs and brush until the greenhouse came into sight. Most of the ceiling panes were intact, though a few had been broken out by growing plants that now towered above the rest of the structure. For all the dead things around it, Helen could make out the unmistakable green of living things through the filthy glass.

She ran the last few steps and pushed through the doorway, edging around the trunk of an overgrown beech tree that had been a sapling the day before.

The building felt both too-large for its exterior and absolutely cramped. The well-kept plants she'd seen were now firmly in two categories: those who'd survived the absence of Luciana's magic, and those who hadn't. Most of the small flowering plants had died out, but many of the larger species had thrived. She stepped through a thick, two-foot high patch of greenery and was surprised by the powerful scent of fresh mint. Looking down, she plucked a leaf and held it to her nose. It *had* to be mint, there was no question.

She realized that much of the open ground was filled with mint, dandelions, and other hearty ground cover that she didn't recognize. For all its wildness, Helen found herself smiling for the first time since arriving. Here was something *alive*, and what's more - something left of Luciana.

She continued in, past a short, stout, apple tree, through a thorny briar of blackberries, and under a now towering willow on her way to the pond. At least, she was fairly sure she was going the right direction.

It's one building. A Box. How can you manage to get lost?

"Quiet please," she muttered. "I don't need your commentary."

You mean your commentary?

"Shut up."

Desperation grew, and Helen could feel a pressure growing in her chest as her desire to find the pond became a *need*. Her heart was pounding and she knew that, if only she could get there, she could suppress the panic attack that had been building since the moment she stepped across the bridge.

"Damnit," she shoved aside another leafy branch. "I know this fucking-"

She suddenly found herself at the edge of a small clearing, one she recognized immediately. The workbench was in good repair, aside from some moss and a few flushes of mushrooms, but most of the tools were badly rusted. The clay pots scattered around were in fine condition, many of them were full of standing water from rainstorms and leaks from the ceiling. The flagstones were perforated with moss and creeping vines, and the ceiling above was cracked and darkened by moss and dirt, but the area was more than bright enough to reveal the two pots sitting front and center in the workbench.

Helen recognized the pots, but not the plants now sprouting from them. For a moment, she could see herself standing at the bench side by side with Luciana. She relived the experience of planting those seeds and of watching Luciana fully enraptured in one of her passions up close.

Wake up Helen, she's gone.

She blinked and the world was back to normal. Her lover was not here, they were not enjoying an intimate moment where Helen learned about the elements of life. No, instead, Helen was staring at perhaps the only thing that looked as it *should*.

She stepped forward, approaching the bench in quiet awe. Out of each pot had grown a column of thick, thorny vines. They'd arched together, finding one another and entwining until it was impossible to distinguish between the two. This... *merger* of the two plants resulted in a knot of vines that was completely covered in small roses, and topped with a single vivid rose blossom of the deepest scarlet.

Helen reached out gingerly, touching the petals to reassure herself the thing was real, and marveled at the velvety smoothness. She looked upward, finding a crack in the ceiling directly above the plant, and as she did, she was graced with a bright, warm sunbeam. She closed her eyes and relished the warmth of the light on her face until it faded again.

"I wasn't sure you'd come back."

Helen whipped around, certain the voice was only in her head.

Luciana was standing there, her hair pinned back and her normal attire replaced by khaki shorts, a white blouse, and a pair of rugged looking hiking boots.

"Are you... real?"

Luciana smiled weakly, and nodded.

"I am, Helen," she adjusted a brown leather backpack she carried. "I'm sorry to disturb you, I was just going. I just, well, I wanted to see the greenhouse one more time I suppose. Sorry."

Luciana turned around and took a step back into the jungle of the greenhouse.

"Wait!"

The woman froze mid-step, then turned back.

"Please," Helen took a step forward. "Please, just, wait."

Luciana said nothing but moved back into the clearing facing her.

"I read your note."

"I really am sorry, Helen," Luciana looked at the ground. "I was selfish and cruel."

"I've never had someone act selfishly because they wanted me around," Helen shrugged. "Generally, it's just the opposite."

"I *do*," Luciana stepped forward as well, closing the distance between them to just a few feet. "I do want you around."

Careful.

"What you told me about the Fae and deals," Helen struggled to keep from embracing the woman. "About promises. How they have to keep them? That was true?"

"Every word."

"Can you promise me you won't do that again? That you won't *mislead* me like that?"

"I promise," Luciana blurted her answer out before Helen even finished talking.

"What happened to this place?" Helen's voice was barely over a whisper and she couldn't tear her eyes away from Luciana's.

"I left," she sighed. "And my magic left with me, so it aged. It... caught up."

Helen's mind raced, and a hundred questions got jumbled in her throat at once, leaving her silent, practically vibrating with tension.

"Why did you come back?" Luciana lifted her hand and gently cupped Helen's cheek.

"I don't know," Helen whispered, enthralled in the warmth of the woman's touch. "I just... I guess I realized I didn't know why I was going home either, and of the two..."

"Yes?"

"Of the two, I choose you."

Helen's cheeks flushed nearly as red as the rose behind them and she gulped, waiting for the inevitable hammer fall. Instead, Luciana stepped close enough to wrap her powerful arms around Helen's waist, pulling her close and looking down into her face.

"I…," Luciana bit her lip with uncertainty. "I'd like to kiss you now."

Helen couldn't speak, but she nodded fervently until Lucina interrupted her with a deep, passionate embrace. Their lips met and Helen could taste honey and rosado on the woman's tongue. Luciana's lips were smooth and full, her tongue warm, talented, and ever-so-slightly rough as it danced with her own.

"Does this," Helen broke away for air. "Does this mean you choose me too?"

"Mmmhmph," Luciana answered, their lips already locked once more.

The taller woman reached down and lifted Helen up with an ease that made her burst out in laughter as she locked her knees around the woman's hips.

"*God* you're strong!"

"Must be that gym," Luciana winked, leaning forward for another kiss.

"Wait," Helen set her hands on Luciana's shoulders and looked around, a sudden sadness returning to her heart. "What... what'll happen to this place?"

"Whatever you want," Luciana raised an eyebrow quizzically. "Didn't you read the note?"

"Well, right," Helen frowned. "And we're going to talk about *that*, but I mean, it's gonna be hard to live here... isn't it?"

"Oh, Helen, I..."

"'Oh Helen' what?"

"Helen, I'm not staying here," Luciana was searching her eyes like a lighthouse seeks out ships in a storm. "I meant what I wrote, I'm leaving."

"You're *leaving*? But I'm here now, I'm back!"

"Helen, I've been hiding here for far too long," Luciana smiled. "*You* reminded me of that."

"But-but," Helen sputterred. "But what about me?"

Here it comes.

"Honestly?"

"Yes..."

"I'm uh...," Luciana looked nervous for the first time since they'd met. "I'm hoping you'll come with me."